Opposites Collide

*a twist on Romeo and Juliet
set in our hybrid world*

Day S. Grant

Untangling Words Press

Line Editor: Kelly Helmick of Dog Star Creative Co

Copy Editor: Brit of BookishB Editing

ISBN: 978-1-966242-03-1

eISBN: 978-1-966242-02-4

Contents

Author's Note

Opposites Collide is a cozy detective story that is a twist on *Romeo and Juliet.* You can expect some romance, but this is not a steamy tale. This story is connected to *The Mavens,* but can be read as a standalone. In *The Mavens,* you will see some of the characters, actors, and the movie referenced.

Prologue

Kim

2035

Outside her on-campus apartment, Kim Elliot squeezed the strap of her purse, letting the edges dig into her palms, and tried to look less petrified than she actually was. This was a date. Plenty of people went on dates. She just needed to breathe slowly and remain calm, even if she'd had a crush on Bill Nolan for the past two years. He had been a fellow student in her Sculpture I class, and they hadn't had any classes together since. What he was doing in that class as a history major, she'd never asked as she rarely worked up the nerve to speak to him. In her humble opinion, Bill was the best-looking cat on campus.

She tried not to freak out about the fact that she was more drawn to fellow cat hybrids than any other demographic. Secretly, she wondered if going through puberty after the Crisis when everyone changed — literally — had affected her preferences. When she and her dad had fused with their family's pet Persian cat and joined the ever-growing population of hybrids around the world, she had had bigger fish to fry. Like the issue that pets could only save up to two of their owners. Her mom had had a fifty-fifty chance at surviving the Crisis since they didn't have another pet to save her. She died a few weeks later. Kim wasn't the only person to lose a family member, not by a long shot, but being an active part of global loss didn't make it any easier.

As the years wore on, more than once, Kim had silently bemoaned that her dad had gotten them a *Persian* cat. Having long, thick fur burst from her skin every time she got nervous or someone scared her was less than ideal. But it wasn't as bad as what happened to her nose. Most cat hybrids either had no physical change to their face beyond a thin layer of short fur, or maybe their face changed minutely to give them the slightest bit of a muzzle. When Kim shifted, on the other hand, she looked like someone had punched her and smashed her nose in. She tried to stay in her human form as much as possible for that specific reason — even in Granberg, which was more accepting of people being in hybrid form than her hometown.

Bill was more confident than she was. He was almost always in his hybrid form. His sleek, blue-gray fur was short and set off his green eyes. Kim had seen him in his human form a few times and wondered if he dyed his hair that same blue-gray or if it carried over from his hybrid form. She was thankful that her hair wasn't the same, yellow-streaked off-white that her fur was. Instead, her hair was dark brown. When she shifted, it looked tarnished and weird on her head since it didn't blend well with the rest of her fur. She had no idea how she'd caught Bill's eye.

Kim took one last deep breath as Bill's burnt orange, two-door sports car rolled up in front of her. He got out of the car and hurried around to open her door before she could reach for the handle. Shyly, she smiled and thanked him. His vertical pupils widened a little, and the corners of his eyes crinkled with his smile. Kim's heart beat faster. She slid into the front seat and refocused on her breathing, trying to crush the butterflies in her stomach that threatened to force her to shift.

In the car, a faint honey smell wrapped around her, instantly soothing her and putting her a little more at ease. Her handsome date settled back into the driver's seat and took them out to the main road. Then, he reached over and threaded her fingers through his, even though this was their first date.

"Tell me about your Senior Gallery show," he practically purred at her.

Letting the honey smell that was clearly coming from Bill himself fight the rest of her nerves, she babbled about her portfolio project. All art majors were required to take part in what Granberg University called a Senior Gallery. Her contribution was a mixture of sculptures and canvas paintings. She didn't know what she was going to do with her art degree when she graduated in a few weeks, but that was just another thing that she was trying not to panic about.

"I don't think I heard what history specialization you chose," Kim said, hoping she could get him talking for a bit. She wanted out of the spotlight. Granberg University's quirk of having undergrads take at least four classes focused on a specialty was an easy segue.

"I went with the dual specialization of the 90s and teaching."

"Teaching?"

"Yeah, I volunteered at the local high school the past two summers and worked with their summer school students. I loved helping them overcome learning hurdles. It also let me tap into my creative side by finding new ways to reach students who would rather be anywhere else."

Kim nodded. That must have been why he took the sculpture class. Because he enjoyed creating. She remembered from class that he wasn't, however, particularly talented, at least not at sculpture.

"And the 90s?" she prompted.

"My parents grew up then. They have always waxed poetic about the decade, and I ended up with a fascination for it."

Bill pulled into the local theater and parked.

"I know we said we'd choose the movie when we got here, but I managed to grab tickets to *Opposites Collide*," he said, taking her hand again when they were out of the car.

"They've been sold out for weeks!"

"I know a guy," Bill whispered like it was a secret.

While a remake of Shakespeare's *Romeo and Juliet* didn't sound like it'd be a box office hit, it was the first fully hybrid-centric movie since the Crisis hit fifteen years ago. Most of the world still tried to suppress their hybrid forms, and the movie industry had followed suit. It was rare for people to feel comfortable in their fur, feathers, and scales.

Kim vibrated with excitement. Every critic and review raved about the movie.

Bill showed their tickets at the door and bought them popcorn with catnip-infused butter, which made Kim's mouth water. When they reached their seats, he put his arm over the back of her chair and raised a questioning eyebrow at her as if to ask if that was okay.

She blushed and let herself snuggle in under his arm. It wasn't long before the previews ended and the movie started.

The opening scene panned through people around the globe shifting and living as hybrids. Some looked uncomfortable in their new skin like Kim, but others seemed to embrace their new existence like Bill. While these different hybrids were shown, a voiceover set the scene:

The Crisis hit in 2020 and changed the human landscape. Permanently. The majority of people left alive aren't completely human anymore. After fifteen years, everyone is still figuring out who and what they are.

For those who were adults during the Crisis, their secondary forms often feel strange and disconnected from who they are. They aren't animals, even if they can now shift into humanoid forms of the pets who saved them. Others take such pride in their hybrid forms that new alliances have formed and new discriminations hook their talons into people. The status quo has shifted quickly but hasn't settled as the younger generations continue to grow up.

For those who were kids during the Crisis or born afterwards, their hybrid forms are taking a deeper root. It's not that their animal instincts rule them, but their hybrid forms show through a little more when they wear their human skins. Having two skins is normal for them. Just a fact of life. Still, it's a note of maturity to have complete control of their shifting because they can choose how people see them. For many of these new adults and teens, the pressure of perception imposed by their parents is a difficult burden to navigate. The more polarized their parents' views on being a hybrid are, the harder it is to break free and be who they want to be.

These new aspects of the world have no better example than the Montagues and the Capulets. Both families are supremely proud of their hybrid forms, just as they had been proud of their purebred show pets before the Crisis.

***

Kim hoped the heavy-handed voiceover didn't continue through the rest of the movie but appreciated how it set the scene and reflected the moment they lived in. She popped a piece of the catnip-butter popcorn into her mouth, and Bill squeezed her shoulder as the screen zoomed in on one city. On one hybrid. On the corgi hybrid that had been cast as the new Romeo.

Chapter 1

Miles

Miles Montague ducked into an alley a few blocks away from his family's neighborhood and shifted from his corgi hybrid form to his human one. The extra floof on his chest receded, as did the short fur all over his body. His ears slid down the side of his head and changed into normal, human ears. The sensation of drying tickled his nose as his mini muzzle eased in.

He and his parents were corgi hybrids. His family had been dog breeders on the side for generations before the Crisis hit; now, they prided themselves on how their hybrid forms echoed the most desirable traits of their "breed's standard." In Miles's case, his chest floof, coloring, ears, and smile made him an even more perfect representation of a corgi than his parents. While most people chose their form by how they were feeling or opted to stick with their human form the majority of the time, Miles didn't have the option to choose. It was a point of family pride to stay in their hybrid forms *all* the time. Miles had mastered shifting by the time he turned thirteen rather than between seventeen and twenty like most people did. Between being moguls in the sports industry and the family quirk of always being in their hybrid form, Miles and his parents were easily recognized by sight in Spoville — as were a number of their extended family. At least when covered in fur.

Earlier that day, Miles had carefully chosen what to wear because he didn't want anyone to recognize him. Being in his human form might be enough to hide his identity — no one in Spoville had seen it since before he went through puberty — but he wanted to guarantee anonymity. He picked a pair of old, beat-up blue jeans he'd scrounged up when he went away for college. His red, thread-bare cotton tee-shirt was in better condition than the jeans, but not much; the black decal of a sporty convertible was cracked and faded in many places from multiple washes and being crumpled in his drawer — he had taken perverse pleasure in wearing wrinkled clothes when he was at college.

He hadn't worn the jeans or shirt since he'd moved back to Spoville. Not only did the clothes not fit the family's image, but since starting to work at the family's main office, he wore ironed button-ups with slacks, even though he worked in the sports industry. The ragged ensemble he was wearing was perfect for flying under the radar downtown; no one would give him a second glance. He looked like any other young guy who didn't have big plans for the day, which was exactly who he wanted to be.

He approached the yellow-tinted windows of Insta-Cafe — a cafe that didn't cater to hybrid tastes and was, therefore, frequented mostly by humans. Human-centric areas were few and far between since they only made up twenty percent of the population post-Crisis. Most places had at least some items to whet the newer tastes that came with everyone's changes. Miles glanced around the cafe to check for familiar faces. He didn't see anyone he knew, which was exactly what he had hoped for. He needed a day of just being himself, like he had been able to do at college. Back in his hometown, he had to adhere to the family image and standards. It was exhausting. He didn't want anyone instantly judging him on sight for at least one afternoon.

Some people around the cafe were dressed like him — in old, shabby clothes — but others wore trendy outfits that made them look like they could be standing in beautifully-lit shop windows. One person, in particular, caught Miles's eye. Her long, blonde hair tumbled around her shoulders in loose curls. She wore a short-sleeved, white, button-up blouse with pink and black checkered pants. She even had a silky black scarf tied around her neck that matched her shiny black heels. A pair of big, round, bug-eye sunglasses perched on her face while she sipped a steaming hot drink at one of the outdoor cafe tables. She was straight out of a movie from the 90s.

Normally, Miles avoided hybrids that dressed like her. They often had a connection to his family's nemesis — the local cat-hybrid family, the Capulets. A human, though... they wouldn't necessarily have those connections. Nothing she wore hinted at her being a hybrid in human form. No oddly shaped openings for wings or dorsal fins. No stretchy shoes that could accommodate a different foot shape. As he passed her, he glanced back and saw no obvious tail-hole flaps. She was a breath of pure, antiquated 90s air. And at a cafe that didn't make accommodations for hybrids, she was most likely a human.

Miles made the decision to go directly into the cafe without looking again at the beautiful woman he was dying to talk to; he'd order his drink and then approach. However, as he entered and the pure smell of roasted coffee beans assaulted him, he remembered where he was — at a cafe that catered to humans. None of the typical hybrid-friendly smells accompanied the coffee — no deer syrup, no cricket sprinkles, no underlying smells at all. Just coffee and a hint of chocolate. This cafe wouldn't carry Milk Bone macchiatos, and there was no way he'd drink a plain macchiato. Yuck.

Miles quickly skimmed the menu and ordered a mocha. It wasn't as good as a drink with Milk Bone, but the chocolate would have to do. He was just lucky he could have chocolate; some dog hybrids couldn't handle it. The dark-haired barista smiled up at him and twitched her nose, which made him think that if she wasn't a rodent hybrid, she probably had a close relative who was. Miles had dated a rat hybrid for a few weeks in college, and it had been fun because she knew all the coolest places to go out at night. In Spoville though? No way, no how could he date anyone that wasn't a corgi hybrid or a human. No one else would fit into the family image.

He collected his drink and glanced around at the tables both inside and outside. They all were taken. There were, of course, empty seats at several of them, which fell into his plans perfectly. Now he had an excuse to ask Little Miss 90s to share her table. Leaving the faint cafe music behind and letting a dopey grin take over his face, Miles headed outside; his normal, lovable corgi attitude would do the talking.

Walking right over to Little Miss 90s' table and standing next to the empty chair, he asked, "Hey, do you mind if I join you? All the tables are full." He gestured vaguely around them and gave her a *sorry-but-I'm-really-harmless* smile.

"No problem," she answered after glancing up at him from her e-reader. Her voice was soft and silky to Miles's ears.

Miles sat down on the hard, metal chair, and she watched him through her big sunglasses. He gave her another smile then rested his right ankle on his knee, angling his body out towards the street like he intended to *just* share her table and not bother her. After a moment, she returned her gaze to the book she was reading.

A few bicyclists pedaled by with their wheels making a pleasant whirring noise. Each minute, a handful of cars drove by, their electric motors propelling them forward in near silence. The leaves of the lone tree along the street rustled. Light conversations from other tables and the occasional passersby drifted to Miles's ears.

He split his focus between patiently waiting for his tablemate to pick up her drink again — something white and steaming, a white hot chocolate maybe? — and trying to decide what to do. She seemed about his age, but he hadn't seen her before. He would have noticed her. Perhaps she had moved to the area in the last few years while he was away at school. Maybe she came here to study at the local college. She didn't look like she watched a ton of sports, so she might not know anything about Montague Legacy Sports. That didn't mean she wouldn't know his family though.

Out of the corner of his eye, he saw her take a dainty sip. Her lips molded to the cup as if she were drinking with the Queen. She was pure class and worth the risk.

"My name is Miles," he volunteered once he'd seen her swallow and glance at him rather than her book. He purposely chose not to share his last name. Maybe she wouldn't recognize it, but why ruin things if she did. Even non-sports-focused people in Spoville had a chance of recognizing the name Montague given how often his dad appeared on TV for an interview or commentary of some kind.

She turned to him and tilted her head to the side as if he'd surprised her. While she considered him, his mind scrambled; it occurred to him that Miles wasn't the most common of names. If she'd heard of his family, she might be able to identify him and default to all the assumptions people made about him. That would taint all their interactions. He took a sip of his mocha to cover his racing thoughts, but a sip could only last so long.

Finally, the left side of her lips kicked up a little, and she said, "I'm Jenny."

Without meaning to, Miles's face fell into a goofy grin that he'd been told over and over was "oh so endearing." In all honesty, it was a corgi smile, just on his human face. No one was immune to it.

"Is the book you're reading any good?" he asked.

Jenny reached up and pulled off her big sunglasses, revealing a pair of smiling brown eyes. She leaned forward ever so slightly, but Miles saw it and uncrossed his legs to do the same. He ignored the rough latticed metal of the chair grating through the worn material of his jeans.

"It is, but I find a lot of pre-Crisis stories have interesting takes on the world."

"They really do," he agreed. Miles's most compelling assignments in school had always included comparisons to social issues from the past that either seemed wildly outdated just fifteen or twenty years later or so on the nose about current issues that he couldn't believe the books and articles were published pre-Crisis. "What's grabbing your attention most about this story?"

After they talked about her book, Miles eased them into other topics, asking her questions and leaving her plenty of opportunity to ask her own. When questions struck too close to home, Miles gave evasive answers. He shared that he'd moved into an apartment over near the stadium a year ago. He left out that he'd moved *back* to Spoville and that his family owned the whole apartment complex and the adjoining hotel where all the visiting sports teams stayed. He did mention that he worked in the sports industry but left out that he worked for Montague Legacy Sports and the fact that he was *the* Montague legacy, as his parents never let him forget.

He noticed Jenny gave vague answers on most personal topics as well, but it was only safe for a woman meeting a random guy to do that, so he understood. She shared that she could walk to downtown from her place, which didn't tell Miles much about where she lived. Downtown was rather large and what each person considered walkable varied. She mentioned that she had gone to college locally and now worked at a luxury boutique. The latter detail was a concern. There were several dozen of them downtown, so it was possible she had no connection to either of the Capulets' clothing brands — Birman Folds and Scot's Byss — but she would definitely know of them. If she knew any of the Capulets personally, she wouldn't even talk to him once she knew his last name.

Miles silently admonished himself for overthinking things.

What mattered most was that her answers were smart, and he wanted to see her again. He wanted to talk with her more, about everything. But he felt dishonest, actively hiding his connection to his family; the more they talked, the more his evasive answers bothered him. He didn't want to start off with secrets or lies of omission. While he wasn't sure he wanted to tell her his last name yet, he wanted to be transparent about how his family factored into his life. He didn't want to have to downplay things with her.

"Do you have family in the area?" Miles asked after they'd run through their favorite pre-Crisis movies. They'd both almost finished their drinks, and it made sense that one of them would leave soon. He needed to make sure she knew he wanted to see her again before it was too late.

"Family in the area?" she echoed. A sweet smile spread across her face that made Miles think she found him amusing, and Miles forced himself to look her in the eye as he waited for her response. "Oh yeah. A lot of family."

"Me too," Miles offered before diving in with something he never talked about with anyone. Quietly, he said, "It's a lot of pressure to have everyone's expectations on you." He squeezed his lips together after he said that, his chest constricting a little at his admission.

Jenny's face softened, and Miles could swear he saw surprised understanding in her eyes.

"It's not much fun, is it?" she replied just as quietly. Her gaze drifted off to the street for a moment.

"Do you have them too? A lot of expectations placed on you, that is." Miles focused intently on her, waiting on her next words as if everything depended on them, and weirdly, he felt like everything *did* hang on her response.

"Yeah, Miles. I do, too," she confided. Her eyes met his, and he knew she hadn't told anyone that before either.

"Do you think—" Miles swallowed hard, "you might want to grab dinner with me sometime?" He watched panic flit through Jenny's eyes before they darted from side to side as if checking if someone was watching them.

She licked her lips before whispering, like she didn't want to be heard, "I'm not sure it's a good idea."

Disappointment crashed through Miles. He felt like the kicked puppy he was. Trying not to let it show, he started to give her a small, forced smile.

"—but I want to," she finished even quieter.

Beaming at her, Miles didn't care that he looked like someone had given him his favorite bone. She wanted to see him again. That was all that mattered. He barely noticed the bitter taste of the dregs of his mocha as he took the last sip.

"Here," he pulled his phone out and passed it to her unlocked, not hiding his eagerness to be able to contact her. "Put your number in."

She slid her hand over the table, again like she was trying not to be seen, and Miles suddenly wondered if he should have dressed better. Maybe she was embarrassed to be seen with him. She did look like she should be in a magazine. Obviously, he would dress nicely when he took her to dinner, but she didn't know that. Still, she took his phone and put her number in. Miles watched her hit save when she finished.

"There you—"

His phone buzzed in her hand, cutting off her sentence.

Her eyes widened as she stared at it, clearly reading whatever message popped up whether she intended to or not. Horror, pain, and then finally tears filled her eyes. All in a split second.

Miles had no idea what the message said. What had his family sent him? It had to be them. He wanted to snatch his phone out of her hand and see what had upset her, but he also didn't want to do anything to make the situation worse. He reached out for his phone slowly, as if any action might startle her. When his hand neared hers, her eyes snapped to his.

"I have to go," she said, frantically shoving his phone into his hand as if it had burned her. Then, she grabbed a little black bag he hadn't noticed before and literally ran away from him. Or the table. Or the cafe. Maybe she wasn't running from him, specifically.

Shaking off her reaction, he flipped the phone around and opened the message that was, of course, from his dad.

> Come to Felix's Corner immediately. Aunt Lucy was found dead with that mangy Capulet Walsh. You know those flea-bitten cats are going to try to convince the detectives that Lucy is the reason their street cat is dead.

Miles couldn't breathe. The bitter taste of his last sip came back to him in force.

Aunt Lucy was his favorite aunt and his only blood relative that wasn't a *purebred* dog hybrid. She'd been saved by a corgi-golden retriever mongrel from one of their rare botched breeding ventures. His dad, Aunt Lucy's brother, had never understood why Aunt Lucy had loved those "worthless" pups as much as any purebred and insisted on keeping one. If anything, his dad's stance that non-purebreds were beneath them had gotten stronger after he fused with one of his beloved corgis during the Crisis. Aunt Lucy, on the other hand, didn't demand perfection from anyone. Miles had always felt like she was on his side no matter what. But now, she was gone, and he was completely on his own.

Feeling like a sack of bricks, Miles stood up, shifted back into his corgi hybrid form, not caring if anyone saw him anymore, and walked to the curb. In a mental fog, he held his hand out and summoned a taxi. One stopped; he got in and gave the destination. The taxi pulled away from the curb, and Miles stared out the window unseeing.

When the taxi driver pointed out that they'd arrived, Miles blinked several times; his eyelids scraped over his dry eyes. Forcing himself to function, he focused on what awaited him outside.

Almost a dozen of his family members were outside the run-down cottage that was Felix's Corner. They were yelling so loudly at the group of cat hybrids standing on the other side of the entrance that it sounded like they were barking mad. A police officer stood between the two families, preventing anyone from going inside the tea cottage where Miles assumed his aunt's body was. He swallowed down the litany of horrors that flitted through his mind; Aunt Lucy might not even look like herself anymore. He hoped he wouldn't have to see her body if it was mutilated in some way.

There, over with the elegantly dressed cat hybrids, looking at him apologetically over tear-matted brown and beige cheeks, was a Birman cat hybrid in a white button-up blouse, pink and black checkered pants, black heels, and a jaunty black scarf.

Jenny.

Jennifer Capulet.

The morning replayed in his mind. The surprised look when he'd shared his name and asked her for hers, proving he didn't know who she was. The vague answer about working for a luxury company, making sure she didn't tip him off to who she was. The sweet, amused smile when he'd asked if she had family around, reaffirming that he hadn't figured out who she was.

She, on the other hand, had known who he was the whole time — it was written all over her face.

He was a fool.

But then again, she'd also known exactly what he meant about family pressure. She was experiencing it, too. *And*, she had wanted to see him again even knowing he was a Montague.

Miles sighed, paid the taxi driver, and climbed out to go join his family.

None of that mattered anymore. Not with his aunt dead.

Chapter 2

Poppy

Detective Poppy Barrdom's beak tipped down at the corners as she tried to frown at the missive on her phone. But like most bird hybrids, her beak wasn't very expressive. She wasn't disgruntled because being sent to a double homicide landed outside of her wheelhouse. It wasn't. She was disgruntled because Captain Starl included a note that he was pairing her up with another detective — not her partner — and didn't tell her who. He'd likely overlooked the detail due to the urgency of the situation: Walsh Capulet was dead.

Walsh was a highly respected member of the Capulet family and the CEO of the Capulets' secondary luxury clothing brand, Scot's Byss. Personally, Poppy found Scot's Byss's style more versatile than the family's primary brand, Birman Folds, even if the latter was more coveted. His family would be itching to claw out the perpetrator's eyes — whether literally or metaphorically, only time would tell. She had no idea how they'd respond to one of their own being murdered, even though she was their *preferred* detective; they had enough pull in the area to request who handled their cases. They liked having consistency and to work with a detective that fit their image standards, even if she wasn't a cat hybrid.

It just would have been helpful to know *who* she'd be working with on the case so she could lay groundwork with the Capulets; they hadn't fully come around to accepting her partner Victor Towers after two years. He'd made the mistake of not wearing either of their brands the first time he'd met them. Rather than waste any more time wondering at the situation, Poppy flipped her sirens on and sped over to Felix's Corner to provide the prompt response the Capulets associated with her.

Felix's Corner wasn't a place she'd been before, but she had driven past it several times. She hadn't had a reason to visit any of the tea cottages in the precinct yet. They weren't go-to crime locations. It did strike Poppy as odd that a Capulet — any Capulet — would be found at the only tea cottage in Spoville that catered specifically to humans. As a rule, Capulets frequented hybrid-owned establishments, preferably ones owned by fellow cat hybrids and definitely not any owned by dog hybrids if at all possible; there was a long-standing dislike between them and the Montagues who were a prominent local dog hybrid family in the sports industry.

Furthermore, this specific tea cottage was an even odder location for a Capulet since it was more than a bit rundown. The thatching on the roof was serviceable but faded rather than shining like freshly cut hay. The stucco walls were no longer a bright cream, but a mixture of beige and gray from slipshod repairs that had been slapped on without a care to the previous stucco color. Poppy doubted that Felix's Corner's interior had fared better than the façade. This location didn't make sense. The Capulets displayed such a penchant for luxury that everyone in Spoville knew them as snobs, even if they wanted to be like them — the Capulets were basically local celebrities. Why had Walsh come *here*?

Alarm pulsed through Poppy as she rounded the corner and saw the tea cottage in question. In front of Felix's Corner's pathetic, sagging porch were two large groups standing around an overwhelmed officer whose partner was likely inside and didn't know he needed help. The group to the left's shouts sounded more like growling and barking than actual words; they looked nothing like the good-time group of corgi and golden retriever hybrids that the Montagues were known to be. The group on the right's higher-pitched yells trended a little toward hissing and yowling; the Capulets present had lost the reserved demeanor they purposely displayed to the world. Her fists tightened on the wheel so much that she could swear she heard the soft feathers on her palms crinkle.

Poppy threw her car into park and leaped out.

"Let us in there!" a golden retriever hybrid growled at the officer in front of the door.

"If you let them in, you have to let us in," one of the cat hybrids snarled.

A flap of her feathered arms landed her a few yards from about fifteen Capulets — a full family mix of Birman, Scottish Fold, and Abyssinian cat hybrids.

Poppy hooted loudly to get everyone's attention as a deep voice off to her left bellowed, "Quiet!" and all eyes turned towards her or the bellow.

Poppy looked over at the owner of that low bellow and saw Detective Apollo Pinon. He'd been in the Spoville Police Department longer than she had, but the two of them had never worked together, and, in all honesty, she thought he avoided her. She'd never heard a squeak out of him, much less a bellow. She assumed whatever mouse instincts he had told him to steer clear of her. Mice and owls didn't play well together in the wild after all.

To exacerbate the issue, he wasn't a white or multicolored fancy mouse. He was a dingy gray mouse that actually caused Poppy to salivate a little, which never happened to her with people who had been saved by science lab mice during the Crisis. Poppy purposely avoided thinking about what her reaction signified.

Detective Pinon was dressed in black jeans and boots with a police blue polo shirt, which was a little too relaxed for him to have been on duty like Poppy was when Captain Starl reached out. It made sense that Captain Starl would call Detective Pinon even if he was off duty. As the other ridiculously powerful, semi-celebrity family in the area, Poppy knew Detective Pinon was the Montagues' requested detective. The Montagues and the Capulets were the only people in Spoville who were finicky — and had enough clout to be humored — about which detectives worked their cases.

Oh no. The other victim must be a Montague. And given how the two families were going at it, they blamed the other for the homicides.

"Would all the Capulets please step over here?" Poppy extended a feathered hand to the right and walked several yards away from Detective Pinon and the Montagues.

"Montagues," Detective Pinon bellowed a little quieter than the last time. "If you'd come this way." Poppy saw him wave off to his left and head that way.

Both groups took a second to glower at each other. Then, the Capulets pivoted as one; half of them sauntered, making it look like it had been their intention to move away from the Montagues the whole time, and the other half prowled with a mixture of anger and distraught grief. The Montagues turned away as well. Some of them bounded toward Detective Pinon, while others shuffled their feet with their tails between their legs.

What Poppy wanted to know was how the families got there before her and Detective Pinon. Thankfully, they hadn't made it inside to the crime scene. The pair of officers, who had arrived before Apollo and herself, had made it there in time to secure the scene before the two families descended on the place. The officer that the families had been yelling at must have come out to deal with them while his partner stayed inside the tea cottage to talk with the owner of the establishment or to cordon off the main crime scene as it hadn't even been a full hour since dispatch received the call.

"I know Walsh was a treasured member of your family," Poppy began. She heard a few sniffles at her comment. "Detective Pinon and I will do everything in our power to find out what happened here today."

"Detective Pinon?" Charles Capulet, Walsh's brother, hissed. The portions of his long, beige fur not covered by clothes stood on end while he spoke. His tail, which was twice its normal size, whipped back and forth. He narrowed his eyes, and his lip curled, scrunching the dark markings on his face together. Even his dark-tipped ears were pinned back. He belonged to the prowling and angry faction of the family. In his expensive black suit, he cut an intimidating figure, but Poppy didn't become a detective by wilting in front of aggressive hybrids.

"He's in the Montagues' pocket. He's going to make it look like Walsh is the guilty party even though he's dead!" Over Charles's shoulder, Poppy saw Jennifer, Charles's daughter, flinch at the accusation and glance toward the Montagues as if she felt sorry for their family as much as her own. She, at least, didn't harbor ill-will toward the dog hybrids.

"Detective Pinon is an exemplary detective," Poppy said in her sternest voice, which she'd been told sounded like it belonged to the scariest of schoolteachers, but she couldn't complain because it grabbed everyone's attention. "You know me and my reputation. To insinuate that my colleague or I would allow anyone to get in the way of the truth is insulting and below you." She'd never used this tone with the Capulets before, which was why she added that last part alluding to their lofty place. It wasn't a putdown, but rather a reminder of their own status.

Charles looked mollified, and his ears perked up an inch.

"We know you do good work, Detective Barrdom. I didn't mean to give offense. We trust you to keep an ever-watchful eye on the situation." Charles cast a baleful look at the Montagues *and* Detective Pinon which didn't leave it to the imagination who he thought needed watching.

"And I will," Poppy assured him, ignoring the insinuation and making it clear she was by staring him down with her big, unblinking owl eyes. "I need to confer with Detective Pinon and go inside to do my job. I will be in touch. Don't feel compelled to stay here. I suspect that Detective Pinon and I have much work ahead of us."

"Of course," Charles said, but he made no move to leave. None of the other Capulets appeared inclined to leave either.

Suppressing a sigh, Poppy walked towards the front door of Felix's Corner while smoothing a hand down her silky shirt to brush off the excessive attitude the Capulets seemed to have that day. She gave a nod to the officer who'd held the two families back and told him he did a good job. He was either human or in his human form. Poppy didn't remember his name, but she knew he was new to the department. She let her eyes telegraph that what he'd done was not an easy job.

Once on the rickety porch, she stopped and glanced over at the Montagues where Detective Pinon was gesturing toward her and probably saying something much like what she had told the Capulets. Whatever he said must have been enough because he turned and confidently strode her way.

Maybe he *wasn't* afraid of her.

"Detective Pinon," Poppy said as he approached.

"Best to not look too friendly with each other in front of the families," he advised just loud enough for her to hear.

Poppy stared at him with unblinking, owlish surprise; she had been told multiple times post-Crisis that her stare was discomfiting, but she'd never been able to rid herself of the habit. Deciding she didn't like his *I-know-more-than-you* attitude, Poppy ruffled her feathers in annoyance. For a second, she thought he smiled at her, but she must have been imagining things.

"Let's get on with it," he said in a deep, unhappy voice that easily carried to the two watching families.

"Fine," Poppy answered, letting her annoyance break into her voice, even if it wasn't professional of her to sink to his level. Maybe

Captain Starl had kept them apart because he knew she wouldn't put up with this mouse's arrogance for a second.

Detective Pinon stepped past her and opened the door to Felix's Corner. It creaked like an abandoned building. Poppy thought it was turning out to be more and more of a haunted tea cottage than an idyllic spot for high tea like the sign outside proclaimed. She followed her temporary — very temporary, if she had any say about it — partner inside. He was gentlemanly enough to not slam the door in her face as she entered, but it seemed to be a struggle for him. Before the door swung shut behind them, he had already taken charge of the situation as if he were the official lead in their partnership.

"Where are the owners?" he asked the pretty lizard hybrid officer standing by the staircase directly in front of the entrance. The staircase had crime scene tape across it and clearly led up to the victims since there weren't any dead bodies in the downstairs tearoom.

To the left and right of the staircase, there were a dozen tables spread out over puce carpet that had seen better days. The flowers on the tables were obviously fake, and a few needed to be dusted. There were no lights built into the ceiling and no lamps. The only light came through the grimy windows whose lace curtains drooped under the weight of time as if they felt depressed by their state of affairs. The entire place smelled musty. Poppy wondered how it had remained open and at the fact that she knew Walsh Capulet wouldn't be caught dead there — though he *literally* had been.

"In their house around back," the officer reported back to Detective Pinon. Poppy remembered someone calling her Officer Cane, but she hadn't worked with her on any cases before. Captain Starl had hired the young lizard in the last two or three months, much like her partner outside.

"We should—" Poppy started.

"Any witnesses?" Detective Pinon cut her off as if she had no right to speak.

Officer Cane pursed her lips as she flicked her eyes to Poppy. "None," she said in a tone that implied that she didn't care for Detective Pinon disrespecting Poppy either.

"Okay, head out and help Officer Kent keep the Montagues and the Capulets apart," Detective Pinon continued authoritatively as the angry voices outside punched through the thin cottage walls.

She nodded and headed outside to assist the male officer, who was apparently Officer Kent. Poppy guessed that the two officers had worked with Detective Pinon before.

Poppy watched Detective Pinon continue to ignore her, and she indulged in a small fantasy of snapping his neck with her beak. It wasn't like her beak could fit around his neck. Like most bird hybrids, her beak barely protruded farther than her nose did when in human form. Ripping off one of his oddly large, even for a mouse hybrid, ears was a much more realistic fantasy. Maybe she'd snag a clump of the gray hair on his head and rip a chunk out to add insult to injury.

"Okay, good," Detective Pinon said, spinning around to look at her. He smiled down at her, making her feel like he was more than two or three inches taller than her. Given his conduct, Poppy found the attractive crinkling at the edges of his eyes annoying. "Detective Barrdom, it's nice to officially meet you." He held out his hand like he hadn't been rude and arrogant thirty seconds before. Maybe he had a split personality? "You can call me Apollo when we're alone, of course."

Poppy looked down her beak at the proffered hand with its pale, fur-less fingers, but didn't take it. She raised her feathered eyebrow at him instead.

"Uh…" His mouse tail hesitated mid-swish, and he appeared uncertain. "Do you want to do last names instead? I'm not a fan of being called just Pinon, but if you'd be more… comfortable?"

"What's happening here?" Poppy asked, gesturing between them. Apollo blinked at her so rapidly it made her think of a debutant fluttering their eyelashes despite the fact that he was clearly confused, not flirting.

"What exactly did the captain tell you?" he asked. His head tilted to the side and one of his eyebrows scrunched down a little as he looked at her.

"That there was a double homicide, one of the victims is Walsh Capulet, and that I wouldn't be working with Detective Towers like I normally do."

"No, that's not what I meant. What did he tell you about us?" Apollo gestured between the two of them like they had an *us.*"

Poppy glanced around the empty room, wondering if someone was going to jump out from under a table and reveal… she didn't even know what they'd reveal.

"About us?" she repeated. She stared at his ridiculousness without blinking.

His eyes widened a fraction, and he nodded.

"Honestly, Captain Starl and I have never talked about you. I didn't think it'd be professional to point out that, of everyone in the department, you avoid me like the plague. Likely because you're a mouse hybrid," she added to soften the accusation by giving him an excuse. Given that his mouth now hung slightly ajar, she hadn't succeeded at softening anything.

After a long, silent minute, Apollo's tongue darted out to lick his lips like he was going to speak. Then, he thought better of it and twisted his mouth to the right, setting his whiskers askew in thought.

"Right," he finally said. "When you joined the Spoville Police Department and were assigned the Capulet cases, the captain pulled me aside and laid it out for me. I was to stay as far away from you as possible and give every indication we did not get along. I figured the easiest way to do that, without being openly rude on the regular, was to avoid you."

Poppy's mind ground to a halt. "Why?" she managed to ask.

What did Captain Starl think she'd do to a fellow detective? He'd never expressed any doubts about her. He had given her the impression, in every way possible, that he thought she was extremely competent and trustworthy.

"Because you handle the Capulets and I handle the Montagues," he said as if it explained everything. And maybe it did.

"So, since they hate each other—" her voice trailed off as she thought about it.

"They will trust each of us more if we don't seem too friendly," he finished for her.

Poppy drifted a few steps over to the right and sat down on an unpadded chair at a nearby tea table as she ran through the past few years in her head. Apollo constantly ducking out of the room, or the entire building, when she came in. Her turning a blind eye as if it didn't bother her. Did that send the message that he didn't like her and that she thought he was beneath her notice? Who even monitored such things?

"And you thought I knew this?" she asked to confirm.

"Well, yeah." Apollo looked sick at the idea that she hadn't known.

"Okay, then." Poppy fluffed her feathers to shake off the whole thing. In the back of her mind, she took comfort in the fact that she wasn't salivating over a complete jerk. She stood up and extended her hand. "I'm Poppy. When we're not with the families," she amended with a jerk of her head towards the Capulets and Montagues outside.

"Or with our colleagues," he added. His voice didn't sound appeased, but he took her hand and gave it a firm shake that felt more confident to Poppy than he looked.

Chapter 3

Apollo

Apollo followed Poppy up the dim and worn wooden staircase, staring blankly at the peeling varnish that had seen better days. He didn't know how he felt about her assumption that he'd been frightened of her.

Part of him wanted to chew the captain out for not briefing her. She should have known why they had to avoid each other, but he knew the captain would find Poppy's assumption hilarious. No way was Apollo going to give the captain a reason to break out in neighing laughter; he hated being the butt of the joke.

Apollo wasn't even sure he wanted to tell his brother that the pretty detective he'd been ordered to avoid thought he was scared of her. He'd never live it down. His brother would tease him about it endlessly.

When he reached the top of the stairs, the crime scene unfolded before him, and he forced himself to get to work. There were eight more tea tables up here, and the room looked better maintained than the downstairs.

The floor had the same grungy pink carpet, but it wasn't crushed to the same extent as downstairs. The plastic flowers weren't quite as pathetic, and the tables were dust free as if the upstairs was the only part of the tea cottage that currently saw customers with any sort of regularity. Curtains that should be shot and put out of their misery framed the small but open windows. Fresh air and faint bickering from the two families outside drifted in.

Apollo did a double take at the two *human* bodies on the ground by the table in the back right corner. He'd never seen a Montague, or a Capulet for that matter, in their human form. The captain had given him strict instructions to only interact with the Montagues in his hybrid form and to play up his background as a decorated college athlete in order to ingratiate himself to them. He and Poppy were going to have to find out how the two had been identified. The bodies hadn't even been searched yet, so it wasn't from identification cards. For now, he'd work with the assumption that the woman was Lucy Montague but keep an open mind until forensics confirmed it.

He turned his attention to the alleged body of Lucy first. He had met her several times over the last few years he'd worked with the Montagues. She was the black sheep of the family because she was the sole blood-Montague who wasn't a purebred corgi or golden retriever hybrid.

She was also eccentric by the family's standards. She lived by herself in a condo that was a development or two away from the family's stadium and offices. At Montague Legacy Sports, she organized all the events and activities for visiting teams' families. She was as happy-go-lucky as the rest of her family, but she never acted like she was better than others just because she was a Montague. He'd even been around a few times when she'd voiced criticism of her family's breedist attitudes. All that meant to Apollo, though, was that he had a lot more unknowns with her than he might with any of the other Montagues. She was probably the only wildcard in the family.

As a human, her lifelessly pale brown skin had only a few wrinkles to hint at her forty-eight years. Her hair was long and black with a bit of curl to it, a strong contrast to her hybrid form's gold and white strands. It was splayed out around her head like she'd fallen out of the chair that stood in the crook of her bent legs. On the table sat a pot of tea and a single empty teacup. Her clothes were nicer than anything Apollo had seen her in before. Normally, she wore leggings and a chic track jacket, which fit her job in the sports industry and her active lifestyle. Today though, she was wearing jeans that had a designer label peeking out from behind a brown leather belt. She had fashionable brown boots on instead of sneakers. Her two-piece sweater set that was much more Capulet than Montague in style appeared undisturbed. In fact, from his vantage point, Apollo couldn't see any obvious signs of injury.

Beside her lay a man with a slit throat — supposedly a Capulet. His head and torso lay in a smaller pool of blood than Apollo would expect from someone of his size. In the pooled blood was a knife, which they'd be unlikely to get any prints from between the blood covering it and the ridges along the handle. A single, overturned chair was nearby. It could have been knocked over in a struggle.

In his human form, the Capulet was blond and fair skinned. His clothes were fairly nondescript: slightly worn jeans, a black T-shirt, casual black sneakers. Again, not typical of his family from what Apollo knew of them. The Capulets outside were all dressed to the nines and carefully put together even though it wasn't a weekday. From his knowledge, the Capulets were much like the Montagues in that they'd had lucrative businesses for generations and the pricey hobby of breeding show animals, cats and dogs respectively. Each family was ridiculously proud of both their businesses and their pets; each family still bred show dogs and show cats.

Poppy was walking along the edge of the room in little spurts of movement that were common to bird hybrids and made Apollo think of a bird flitting from one branch to the next. He wondered if her feathers were soft like down or stiff like wing feathers or both. She was already trying to get a new angle on the scene and inadvertently showcasing how much the floor creaked. Apollo let his eyes sweep over her one more time than was appropriate; with no one else around, he didn't have to worry about someone blowing his attention out of proportion and it somehow being reported to the Montagues.

Like always, Poppy was well dressed. Her black, heeled boots were practical, but also said she cared what she looked like. The black pants she wore fit her curves in a way Apollo knew he should not be taking the time to appreciate, and her blue top had a frilly detail around the neckline and over her shoulders that fluttered as she moved around. If he had to guess, he'd say she was wearing clothes from one of the luxury brands the Capulets owned — as their detective, it would make sense. Poppy rounded the far side of the bodies and looked over at him just as he started moving his eyes back to the victims.

"What can you tell me about the male victim? Did you have any direct dealings with him? Are you confident he's a Capulet?" Apollo asked quietly to prevent his voice from drifting outside.

"This is Walsh Capulet as far as I can tell." She'd also pitched her voice low to ensure the families couldn't hear them. "I've never seen him in his human form, but he looks much like the photo I saw of him from pre-Crisis media reports. He's Charles Capulet's younger brother by two years." She paused and glanced over at him. "Charles is the head of the family, CEO of their more successful brand, Birman Folds, and the angriest of the cats out front." Poppy focused back on the dead bodies after adding in the extra information for him. "Walsh was the CEO of their secondary brand, Scot's Byss. He was hardworking, and his employees knew he looked out for their best interests, even going head-to-head with his brother to make sure they weren't taken advantage of. I acted as an intermediary on a case for him that involved embezzlement from employee retirement accounts. Unlike his brother who's a Birman hybrid, Walsh was an Abyssinian hybrid and loved the water."

"A cat that liked water?" Apollo asked.

"Abyssinian cats often have that trait apparently, but given his age, it's probable that his love of water didn't come from fusing with his pet cat but was something he already liked." Poppy shrugged her shoulders in a motion that sent her on a little hop through the air. "And the Montague?"

"Lucy is the younger sister of Edward Montague, who's the head of the Montague family and of Montague Legacy Sports. She's a corgi-golden retriever hybrid mix and never fit in great with the rest of the family. I'm working on the assumption that this *is* Lucy;

I don't recall any information about what she looked like in human form. We'll have to double check her identity."

"We'll do that for both of them," Poppy concurred.

"What do you make of the way they're dressed?"

"I've never seen Walsh outside of work hours, but I wouldn't have put him in clothes like this; it doesn't match their brands. I take it that this isn't Lucy's normal attire?"

Apollo shook his head.

"We'll have to make sure to slip in questions about it when we talk to the families," Poppy said after taking a good minute to think. "It's probably connected to them being in their human forms."

They continued to work their way around the scene and fill each other in on what they knew about the respective victims. It didn't take them long to learn all they could without touching anything; that had to wait for the forensics team that would arrive in the next hour.

Out of the corner of his eye, Apollo watched Poppy walk over to the little front window and asked, "Did anyone leave?" He hadn't been trying to listen to the voices outside, but he also hadn't registered a significant change in the number or volume of the voices.

"Yeah. Seven of the Capulets are still here, and there are five Montagues. None of them are any happier about the other group's presence than when we arrived."

Apollo joined her at the window and looked over her shoulder to see which Montagues had stayed. Edward Montague, Lucy's brother, was still there and still seething. His son and heir, Miles, stood beside him and appeared to be hit the hardest by the loss of his aunt. Miles's shoulders were slumped, and his ears had an uncharacteristic droop to them; his look was forlorn rather than raging like the others. His clothes also missed the athletic or business look that the rest of his family wore. The other three Montagues were golden retriever hybrids — two cousins and an aunt perhaps. Apollo didn't know them specifically. They were angry though; one was literally baring their teeth and not in a smile.

"Delightful," Apollo muttered. "Any idea how they found out about the bodies?" Feathers around where Poppy's ears would be if she were in her human form vibrated with his breath. Realizing how close he was standing to her, in a window where anyone could see them no less, he stepped back. He needed to make sure he kept his distance regardless of how much he didn't want to.

"No, but I'm sure none of them will come straight out and tell us; it would look incriminating," Poppy said, turning away from the window. "But it has to be a family member that identified them. My guess? A Montague."

Apollo raised his eyebrow at the accusation, and Poppy lifted a feathered finger to stay any objections.

"I'm pretty sure this is Walsh. He looks much the same as he did pre-Crisis. So someone, in the families or not, could probably recognize him with ease. But identifying Lucy would be more challenging; you already admitted that even you aren't sure this is Lucy, and you've studied the family. You weren't called in for a Jane Doe. Who would know Lucy better than her own family? It's more likely to be a Montague."

Apollo conceded the point. And regardless of who identified them, it wouldn't look good for either the Montagues or the Capulets to admit they knew one or both victims were at Felix's Corner in their rarely used human forms. The fact that both families arrived on the scene almost as quickly as the first officers didn't make either family look innocent.

"Are you ready to talk to the owners and see what they know?" Apollo asked.

Poppy nodded, and they headed downstairs and out back to the small, two-bedroom house that looked just like the tea cottage — rundown. Inside the owner's home, two anxious women sat at a white, scratched-up kitchen table. They both had furrowed brows and looked near tears. Untouched cups of tea sat in front of them. The cabinets behind them had a warped plastic coating that had seen better days. However, the black-and-white checkered floor was spotless with only a handful of scuff marks. Apollo couldn't tell if the clean smell that suffused the place was that of general cleanliness or evidence of recent cleaning.

"I'm Detective Barrdom, and this is Detective Pinon," Poppy introduced them. The woman on the left tried to smile in greeting, but failed. "We understand you're the owners and the only people present for today's incident?"

"Yes," the woman who had tried to smile said. Her brown, frizzy hair had suffered from seeing two murder victims, likely due to grabbing at it in stress. And her light blue striped blouse and black slacks didn't have any traces of blood on them but were more wrinkled than Apollo might have expected from a business owner. "Patricia and I own Felix's Corner. We were the only ones on the premises, as far as we know. I... I found the bodies." Her hands shook as she spoke, and she pressed them against the table.

"Could we get your full names?" Apollo asked, pulling a notepad out of his back pocket. Was the woman trying to ground herself and stop the shaking or hide the shaking that came from having killed someone?

"Of course," she said with a tremor in her voice. "I'm Tanya Williams, and this is Patricia Echos." Patricia gave a nod at her name. She was smaller than Tanya and looked like she'd just rolled out of bed. Her medium-length, auburn hair hadn't been brushed. She either didn't get much sun or was abnormally pale at the moment. "We recently inherited this place from my Uncle Felix. Felix Carcel."

Apollo wrote down a few notes after their names about their clothes and appearance to make sure that was what they were wearing when Officers Kent and Cane arrived. However, if the two women were involved, they likely would have changed their clothes before any police showed up.

"I'm sorry for your loss," Poppy offered. Apollo mentally noted that Poppy had great bedside manner. "Did you call anyone besides the police when you found the bodies?"

Tanya shook her head with wide, horrified eyes. He and Poppy shifted their eyes to Patricia who also said she hadn't called anyone.

"Were the two victims upstairs regulars of yours?" Poppy asked with an encouraging smile that put the frightened women a bit more at ease.

"I'd never seen the man before," Tanya said, "but the woman has come in two or three times in the four months we've been here."

"I didn't go inside today until after..." Patricia's voice trailed off and she started breathing faster. Tanya made soothing noises and rubbed Patricia's back. "I didn't see the bodies, so I don't know what the man looks like," Patricia finally finished. That confirmed

Apollo's earlier suspicion that she hadn't left the house yet that day. Poppy gave a quick description of Walsh's human appearance and of his hybrid appearance, and Patricia said she didn't think she'd seen him before either.

"During her previous visits, was the woman in her human form like today?" Apollo asked.

The two women blinked at him, taken aback.

"She's a dog hybrid," Poppy explained. "Perhaps she also came by in her hybrid form?" Apollo gave a quick description of Lucy's hybrid form and explained that she had all the traits of a golden retriever hybrid but classic corgi markings; her looks made her stand out among most mixed-breed dog hybrids who strongly favored one breed.

"I've never seen a hybrid that matches that description," Tanya said. "We didn't even know she was a hybrid. We are trying to widen our offerings to get hybrids to come in. You know, adding marrow milk, loose-cricket tea, and fungi steeps. She never ordered any of those."

Apollo heard Poppy swallow at the mention of loose-cricket tea and started a mental file on things Poppy liked that he should probably be ignoring. For himself, he would pick the fungi tea out of those options. It was possible that, as a dog hybrid, Lucy enjoyed marrow milk in her tea, but not all dog hybrids did. Her tea selection didn't necessarily indicate that she was trying to hide her identity. It might not be relevant at all.

"We haven't gotten any hybrid customers yet, at least that we knew of," Patricia added. "Uncle Felix was..." She glanced at her partner.

"Bigoted," Tanya said flatly. "He never accepted hybrids. Refused service if he had an inkling they might be hybrids."

"That must make turning the business around difficult," Poppy acknowledged in the face of Tanya's disgust with her uncle. "This morning, did you notice anything about your two customers? Anything different or out of the ordinary?"

"Well," Tanya said, "the woman was upset when she arrived. I noticed she was more fidgety than normal. But she ordered her normal tea, Lapsang Souchong, and sat at her usual table."

"And what time was that?" Apollo asked.

"She came in around ten thirty. The other days she's come, it's been in the afternoon." Tanya clarified. "When I brought her tea to her ten or fifteen minutes later, she was gazing off and didn't seem to notice me. I popped back here to the house after that to check on Patricia."

"I know Tanya was back here before eleven. I remember the time 'cause I wanted to see how long it had been since I'd last thrown up," Patricia added, and Apollo noticed her hand slide discreetly over her stomach.

"Of course. Morning sickness can really throw off your day," Poppy said, full of understanding. "And the man? When did he arrive? Soon after you went back to the tea cottage?"

"We never saw him or anyone else arrive," Tanya said. She wrung her hands several times until Patricia reached over to calm her.

Apollo and Poppy exchanged a quick glance. It was odd that the owners wouldn't have seen a customer arrive. Tanya could be experiencing guilt about the murders. But the question was if she regretted committing them, letting someone else come in to commit them, or that it happened because she wasn't attentive?

"Would we be able to see the recordings from your security cameras?" Poppy asked. Apollo had forgotten about the three clunky cameras he'd seen — one by the front door, another near the back door with the register and phone, and a third pointing at the house they were in now. The couple's cooperation with the recordings could go a long way in clearing them from the suspect list, but it was too soon to tell.

"We haven't been able to update and fix all three cameras yet," Tanya explained in a hurry. "We've replaced the one that watches the back of the shop to the house, for personal safety, and the one that watches the cash register. The one by the front door is for show until we have the money to get it worked on."

"How long were you back here before you discovered what had happened inside?" Apollo prompted. He wanted to keep them talking. He'd talk to Poppy later to see if she felt the camera situation was understandable or deliberate. The techs also needed to check the front camera to see if what Tanya said was true and it wasn't just turned off.

"Thirty, maybe forty minutes," Tanya said. "The woman was here for maybe an hour by the time I went back inside. She normally comes in for two hours but gets a refill on her tea after about an hour. That's why I went upstairs as soon as I got back to the cottage... and they... they were... dead." The expression on Tanya's face conveyed that the image of the dead bodies upstairs already haunted her. Patricia squeezed her hand.

"I screamed," Tanya managed to say after a minute, "and ran downstairs just as Patricia burst in the back door to see what was wrong. I told her—"

"And I ran into the bathroom to throw up again," Patricia said. She looked like she might need to do just that again.

"I called the police. I wouldn't let Patricia go up and see. I don't want to put her through any unnecessary stress. I insisted she go back to bed and focus on taking care of herself."

"There's no need for her to see the crime scene right now," Poppy agreed soothingly. "We'll be taking photos and, if we need to ask her questions about it, we can show her those then."

"Is it normal for you to leave the tea cottage unsupervised for more than a few minutes?" Apollo asked. Being away for over a half hour didn't seem like a smart thing for revamping a business. He and Poppy would need to see the exact timing of the 911 call and match it with the security footage they got.

"No," Patricia said while Tanya shook her head. Patricia's pale face lost a little more color as she explained: "Tanya tried to get me to eat when she checked on me, and I couldn't keep it down. I didn't quite make it to the bathroom, so she stayed away from the front longer than she normally might to clean things up. That way I could focus on resting." That meant the cleaning products Apollo could smell were from recent use, but the women did supply a reasonable explanation.

"We get so few customers, I didn't think a few extra minutes would make a difference," Tanya whispered. "The ones we do get, seat themselves and take their time picking the tea they want. A few extra minutes in back shouldn't have made a difference." Her voice rose into a plea, like she wanted Poppy and him to assure her she had done nothing wrong.

Before they could go any further, loud barks and a yowl pierced the air — both sounding more animal than human. Then, they heard Officers Kent and Cane shouting out front. Apollo dashed out the door but heard Poppy pause long enough to assure the two women that they would be back soon to finish their conversation and collect the recordings from the two working cameras.

Apollo glanced at the placement of the cameras as he dashed through the tea cottage. He hoped the recordings would at minimum have the sound of the front door closing to pinpoint Walsh's arrival and somehow corroborate Tanya and Patricia's alibis. If all the stars aligned, they'd also hear evidence of the murderer entering and noises of at least Walsh struggling while his throat was cut. Defining the timeline would be key.

When Apollo burst through the front door and onto the rickety porch, he saw Charles Capulet and Edward Montague being pried apart by Officers Kent and Cane. Kent had a nasty looking set of scratches on his biceps that must have come from the bristling cat he was pushing backward. Edward Montague was snapping his teeth over the ripped shoulder of Cane's uniform like he'd gone rabid.

Apollo groaned and hurried over to help Cane with the head of the Montague family. She was a head shorter and at least seventy pounds lighter than Edward Montague; while Cane was impeding his aggressive lunges past her, she wasn't exactly managing to hold him back from advancing. Kent was doing a better job containing Charles Capulet, who had already retracted his claws and was pulling himself together, aware he had injured a police officer.

While Apollo helped Cane, he wondered if Edward had dabbled in steroids prior to the Crisis; it wouldn't be the first time someone in the sports industry partook and would explain his explosive aggression. After a minute, Poppy's voice rang out as she joined Kent and hooted sharp admonishments at the Capulets.

This was going to be a long case.

Chapter 4

Poppy

Poppy checked in the next morning with her normal partner, Victor, to see what he'd been assigned to while she worked with Apollo. She didn't envy Victor. He'd been assigned Apollo's rookie detective training detail until she and Apollo wrapped up the Capulet-Montague case. Poppy was wincing at Victor's recounting of the previous day when Apollo arrived.

"Did you see the IDs came through?" her temporary partner snapped at her before she even saw him.

She turned around. It was clear Apollo woke up on the wrong side of the bed. Not that he looked like it. His appearance was overall the same as the day before — gray all over with ears she could rip off without a second thought if he kept up his current attitude. Today, he'd upgraded from yesterday's polo to a black button-up. For whatever reason, the badge on his belt struck her as arrogant.

"Good morning to you," Poppy replied as if educating a toddler in manners.

Not breaking stride at her work area, he grunted back at her and continued across the room to his own desk.

"Uhh," Victor said beside her.

"Your training detail is looking pretty good right about now, huh?" she muttered to Victor with a roll of her eyes before trailing after Apollo.

Whatever greetings Apollo gave their coworkers as he wove through the desks to get to his own must have been more friendly than his non-hello to her. Many of them smiled at him and replied back. He was already sitting at his desk when Poppy caught up with him.

"Both IDs came back positive?" she asked, determined to be pleasant but focused.

The superior head tilt Apollo gave her seemed to say, "As if anything else could be the case. I'm better than you." Poppy narrowed her eyes at him in annoyance while he pulled up the report on his desk computer.

"With their ages, it wasn't difficult. They were both fingerprinted pre-Crisis, and being cat and dog hybrids, it isn't like their fingerprints changed much when they shifted. Even if they had died in their hybrid forms, we'd have IDed them easily from their fingerprints." Apollo glanced at Poppy's feathered hand on his desk as if to nail his point home.

It had taken ten years post-Crisis to get laws passed that ensured fingerprinting was done in both human and hybrid forms. Poppy was a prime example of why they needed both sets of fingerprints, but also of why fingerprints didn't always work anymore either.

The downy feathers on *her* fingertips, while small, shifted every time she touched a surface; and that was without taking into account that she lost some of them regularly and got new ones. Her hybrid fingerprints only said that a feathered finger had been there. On the other hand, reptile hybrids had scaled fingertips that didn't match their human fingerprints, but their fingerprints were still uniquely the same each time they shifted. The pads of dog hybrids, cat hybrids, and clearly mouse hybrids like Apollo retained their fingerprints most of the time, but shifting occasionally distorted a few. Crime had taken a tricky turn post-Crisis because some criminals would shift so *their fingerprints* weren't at the scene.

"Okay," Poppy said, ignoring the fact that Apollo's glance at her hand had lingered into a stare as she skimmed the ID report. Did he suspect her of wrongdoing because her hybrid form couldn't be fingerprinted? She shook off the ridiculousness of his attitude. Regardless of what Apollo thought of her, the victims were, without a doubt, Walsh Capulet and Lucy Montague. "I have the security recordings from Felix's Corner set up to watch," she finally said, turning away before he could respond.

This time, she made him catch up to her.

When Apollo stepped into the small viewing room, he surprised Poppy by closing the door behind him. Maybe he thought they'd have to turn the volume up really high to hear background noises? It wasn't a completely crazy idea. He plopped down in the chair next to her with a *let's-get-this-over-with* attitude, if she'd interrupted his body language correctly.

"What's your problem today?" Poppy asked, letting her frustration come through in her voice.

She saw Apollo's brow drop as he flicked his eyes over to her.

"Still have windows here," he answered with a sarcastic smile, but in a much more subdued tone.

Poppy's eyes widened to their maximum as what he said sunk in. He hadn't woken up on the wrong side of the bed. He was being an ass to her on purpose because other people were watching and listening. *This* was what he meant yesterday when he said he'd figured avoiding her was easier. Fine then, he could play his game, but she wasn't having any of it.

"You can't seriously think the Capulets and Montagues have eyes and ears in the Spoville Police Department."

He shrugged like he couldn't care less and tilted his head to the side as if *asking* Poppy to tear off his ear. "There were in past years. The captain doesn't want us to risk it." His voice was still at complete odds with his facade.

"Let's watch these videos," Poppy sighed, turning to focus on the screen in front of her.

After two hours of videos, they had learned the following: Tanya Williams was the only person on camera until she screamed off-camera at 11:37. Directly thereafter, Patricia Echos burst through the back door and heard Tanya hysterically reporting the murders to 911; Patricia then dashed into the small bathroom beside the register and phone as she'd said. Tanya had just gotten Patricia to go back to the house to lie down when Officers Kent and Cane arrived. The rest of the information Poppy and Apollo could glean from the recordings was sound based.

A door off-screen opened and shut at 10:35. Presumably, Lucy had arrived. Tanya went back to check on her wife Patricia at 10:52. At 10:58, the same door sound repeated itself. Both times, the door sounded as if it had been slammed. Either Walsh or the murderer had arrived. This new arrival had heavier footsteps that the recording picked up — possibly while going up the stairs. There were a few creaks from the upstairs floor, too. At 11:13, there was a loud thud, immediately followed by a smaller thud; perhaps the knocked over chair. Eight minutes later, a cut off shout ended with a much more resounding thud. Then nothing until Tanya came bustling back in, grabbed a new pot of hot water for Lucy and hurried upstairs to scream at 11:37. Either the murderer or Walsh had been more careful with the front door since they couldn't hear it open and close a third or fourth time.

This gave Poppy and Apollo a thirty-minute time frame to work with, but no clues to who had killed Lucy and Walsh. Since Officers Kent and Cane were assigned to assist her and Apollo on the case, Poppy asked them to go back to Felix's Corner and see if there were any cameras that showed the street or the front of the tea cottage that would help them come up with a suspect list. Kent and Cane were also compiling a list of the order in which the Montagues and Capulets had arrived the previous day. Their help let Poppy and Apollo focus on their next task — looking for connections between Lucy and Walsh that would help them figure out why they were murdered. First up, they needed to check out Walsh's home and then head to Lucy's to see what information they could find.

Poppy thought they could make it out of the police station without making a scene of their "dislike" of one another, but her hopes were dashed when Apollo scoffed loudly at taking her car, berating it for several, petty reasons. At first, it surprised her that he knew what she drove, but her surprise withered when he arrogantly continued to run his mouth. His derision for her vehicle didn't stop until she literally snapped her beak at him as if threatening to take a bite out of him. Then, he insisted they take his car. Poppy couldn't bring herself to argue with him without losing her temper completely. Instead, she silently fumed at him, but ultimately followed him out to the sun-warmed parking lot. She refused to behave as unprofessionally as him.

When she saw his car, Poppy got her first hint as to why he was the Montagues' preferred detective. Her own car was maybe a little luxurious for a police detective, but in an understated way. His car — a souped-up, sporty, silver coupe — was all flash. It was the type of car she expected a Montague to drive, not a police detective. Before climbing in, Apollo shot her a smug, *my-car-is-hot* look that ratcheted up her irritation another notch or two.

They drove in silence for the first ten minutes while Poppy seethed in his oddly cedar-scented car. Logically, she knew he'd berated her car for show, but she *liked* her car. As he pulled out of the parking lot, Poppy silently made a list of all the things wrong with Apollo's car. It was barely street legal and implied that he was on the take because what cop could afford this? The seats were too comfortable. It smelled too nice. He looked too good with his wrist resting on the steering wheel while he drove.

Apollo broke their silence and Poppy's list making by suggesting they grab sandwiches for lunch along the way; nothing about him implied he was irked in the least. Taking a card from his playbook and switching from antagonistic to friendly on a dime, Poppy agreed to stopping for food. She wondered if Apollo could truly turn his arrogance on and off like she'd seen or, if like her, he could do it for show but still seethed inside.

By the time Apollo parallel parked his sporty car outside Walsh's three-story townhouse, Poppy had calmed down. Walsh's townhouse was typical of most pre-Crisis homes. It was light gray with white trim and had a white picket fence around the massive tree that dominated the small lawn. No obvious hybrid modifications stood out — like a porch column turned giant scratching post or extra-large windows to increase the number of sunny spots for basking. Such a benign house for a hybrid was quickly becoming a rarity.

"That's Jennifer Capulet outside the door," Poppy said when she saw the young woman. Today, Jennifer wore all black; her outfit reminded Poppy of the old movie *Funny Face*. The all-black ensemble made Jennifer's off-white fur appear powdered on around the dark seal-point markings on her face and pointy ears. Her long, off-white hair was pulled back into a sleek ponytail. "I'm surprised the family sent her to let us in. Yesterday, she appeared more broken up than most by her uncle's death."

"You should question her. She knows you better," Apollo said, and Poppy almost rolled her eyes.

"And until we know how she is going to react to you, we should be careful about you going anywhere to 'plant' something in her uncle's house."

"Fair point," Apollo muttered.

"Though, yesterday, she didn't seem to harbor any animosity toward the Montagues."

"That'll be a pleasant change of speed."

Poppy smiled at the exasperated comment, and Apollo fixed a pretend glare on her that she returned in character. Maybe she could get used to their fake animosity, but it didn't come naturally to her. They both climbed out of the car then, and while Poppy wouldn't have minded letting Apollo walk in front of her in order to admire his backside, she briskly took the lead. She needed to be the first to reach Jennifer.

"Good morning," Poppy said. "How are you doing today?" She gave Jennifer an honest, concerned look. Jennifer had clearly continued crying after leaving Felix's Corner the day before. The fur around her eyes appeared to be weighed down by traces of salt and looked distinctly crunchy at the moment.

"I'm here." Jennifer's shoulders hitched up and dropped. Her whole body slumped a little.

"It's really helpful of you to come let Detective Pinon and me into your uncle's townhouse."

Jennifer's eyes flicked past Poppy, and she nodded a hello at Apollo.

"We're both very sorry for your loss," Apollo offered. He put aside the gruff act he'd been using around the other officers and the families for the statement, which Poppy noted was well-done of him. No reason to upset the distraught young woman more.

"I need to get some paperwork from Uncle Walsh's desk," Jennifer said, her voice hitching on her uncle's name. "If that's allowed, of course."

"Paperwork?" Poppy asked as Jennifer unlocked the front door.

"I was Uncle Walsh's assistant during college. Since graduation, I've been shadowing him. He was slowly moving more and more of his responsibilities to me. He wanted to retire early and travel," she said.

They all walked inside. The front door opened into a small foyer with black wood floors and light blue walls. The foyer went straight to a staircase that led upstairs to the rest of the place. Before the staircase, an open door on the left led to the garage. The entire area had a chill to it that gave Poppy instant goosebumps, which she hated. Goosebumps puffed her feathers out enough to cause discomfort in her clothes.

"You were lined up to be the new CEO of Scot's Byss?" Apollo's surprise tinted his voice.

Personally, Poppy thought Jennifer was a better match for Scot's Byss than Birman Folds. The Scot's Byss brand was retro, reminiscent of the 90s or earlier, which was how Jennifer always dressed. Birman Folds's style was modern and business oriented. Granted, it was possible Jennifer dressed that way *because* she would be the CEO of Scot's Byss in the future.

"But not for several years," Jennifer hiccupped.

Poppy reached out and rubbed Jennifer's back. Jennifer turned and threw her arms around Poppy's neck, sobbing into her shoulder. Wide-eyed with surprise, Poppy held Jennifer while she cried.

Apollo walked around the two of them and mouthed, "Is this normal?" pointing between Jennifer and her.

Poppy leaned her head away from the sobbing woman in her arms and shook it no, making sure her feathers didn't brush Jennifer's fur or whiskers. She had met Jennifer a few times before. They had officially met when Walsh had asked for police assistance with the embezzlement issue because Jennifer had sat in on one of their meetings. But twice before that when Poppy had given Charles Capulet investigation updates at their house, Jennifer had been around. None of that warranted the woman throwing herself into Poppy's arms. In Poppy's estimation, she was the equivalent of a mere acquaintance or contractor Jennifer's family worked with. Not someone you turned to in despair. Didn't she have someone in her family or among her friends to lean on?

"Who will take over as CEO until you're ready?" Poppy asked quietly, thinking that could be a motive for murdering Walsh, even if it didn't take Lucy Montague into account, or the fact that the two were together at all, which she and Apollo agreed was downright odd.

Jennifer squeezed her harder, and her crying intensified. Behind Jennifer, Apollo flicked his finger at the door to the garage and left Poppy in the foyer with Jennifer. Poppy almost objected to him searching alone, but it was obvious that Jennifer wasn't worried about Apollo planting something to frame her uncle. She had bigger problems than the Montague's detective being around.

"Let's head upstairs and see about finding you some tissues," Poppy said. Jennifer nodded into her shoulder before letting Poppy guide her up the stairs with an arm around her.

The color-scheme upstairs replicated that of the foyer — black wood floors gleamed, and light blue walls merged into windows that lit up the entire open floor plan. The first thing Poppy noticed was a faint olive scent. A cat hybrid friend had once told Poppy that anything olive perked them up and helped them face the day.

Towards the front of the townhouse was the living room with aubergine armchairs and a couch that faced a fireplace with a black mantle. Beyond the living room was a kitchen with shiny silver appliances and midnight blue cabinets. A dining table and chairs disappeared under the staircase that rose up to the third floor.

They walked over to the couches, and Poppy fetched a tissue box from the bathroom Jennifer pointed out past the dining table under the staircase. Once Jennifer had control of her crying, Poppy tried again.

"I'm going to need you to tell me who is going to take over as CEO until you're ready."

"No one," Jennifer gulped. "I start tomorrow."

"You're... twenty-two? Twenty-three? That's a bit younger than normal." Poppy's mind scrambled to find any reason that Jennifer being CEO would factor into Walsh and Lucy's deaths, but she couldn't find any.

"Twenty-two," Jennifer whispered in a voice that agreed with Poppy's assessment.

Apollo joined them upstairs, and Poppy separated herself from Jennifer.

"Two cars in the garage, keys hanging by the door," Apollo said quietly. "Both cars are registered to Walsh, but we'll have a team dust the keys and front seats for prints. We'll need to determine if the murderer returned his car or if Walsh left without it."

Poppy nodded and updated him, "Jennifer's CEO as of tomorrow and not thrilled about the amount of responsibility that's falling on her shoulders."

Apollo frowned at that news, but they both set to searching the second floor of Walsh's townhouse without another word. There was nothing of note in the kitchen cabinets. The trinkets on the decorative bookcase behind the couches appeared benign. Everything was in its place and, if anything, maybe a little impersonal. The living room and kitchen areas were stylish but too slick to live in from Poppy's perspective. Nothing triggered alarms or hinted at what happened to Walsh and Lucy.

"We're going to head up to the third floor and look around. Then, we'll come get you and help you gather what you need from his office, okay Jennifer?" Poppy said. She wanted the young woman to know what they were doing in case she got quizzed about the investigation when she got home.

Jennifer nodded and then stared out one of the windows as if the drifting clouds outside held all the answers.

In front of Poppy, Apollo started climbing the stairs. She wished she was more in the mood to check out his ass on the way up, but Jennifer's crying earlier and the challenges she had ahead of her as a young CEO hadn't left Poppy extra head space for anything but solving the murders.

Halfway up the stairs, Apollo froze. Poppy looked up at him instead of at her feet and saw him cock his head to the left and twitch his overly large right ear. He spun around, eyes wide, and started pushing Poppy back down the stairs.

"What—?" was all Poppy got out before the third floor exploded above them.

The blast threw them back, and Poppy landed hard with Apollo's heavy body on top of her. The impact jarred her so badly she shifted into her human form. Drawing in a gasping breath, the smell of burning honeysuckle overwhelmed Poppy. Wrinkling her nose, she took a few breaths through her mouth as her hands instinctively slid up to check on the dead weight of Apollo. Her hands landed on either side of his abs, and she ignored that he felt incredibly solid. He was probably ripped under his shirt. Her hands slid around to his back, and his shirt seemed intact. He wasn't on fire. Nothing felt wet, so he likely wasn't bleeding.

"Apollo," she whispered.

He groaned, and she felt his head shake, his hair brushing the side of her face. A faint cedar smell from Apollo drifted to her nose through the burning honeysuckle scent. His weight moved on her, forcing what little air she had managed to suck in out of her. His head lifted up from where it hung over her shoulder, and she found herself gazing into steel-gray eyes on a human face she'd never seen up close. He'd shifted too. His mousy gray hair — a color he kept regardless of his form — looked mussed, like he'd just woken up or, in this case, been thrown through the air by an explosion. His lips pulled into an inviting smile and a rough, "Hey," slipped past them. Poppy felt his "hey" through her entire body.

A frightened mew made them both jerk their heads to the living area. Jennifer's dark, pointy ears and dilated eyes peeked out from behind the couch. Jennifer's control impressed Poppy. She knew the Capulets drilled it into their children that they had to be in their hybrid form at all times, and accidental shifts were severely punished. Still, staying in one form during an explosion was not an easy task.

"Are you two okay?" Jennifer managed to ask.

Poppy glanced up at Apollo, seeing in his eyes that he was taking physical stock of his body. "I'm fine," Poppy assured Jennifer and Apollo.

Apollo's eyes focused on her and widened; he'd just realized he was lying on top of her. He jerked off her and onto his knees, steadying himself after the quick movement.

"Yeah," Apollo answered. "I'm fine too."

Then, the sprinklers turned on, instantly drenching them all.

Jennifer hissed, proving she didn't share her late uncle's love of water. Getting up carefully, but as quickly as possible, Poppy and Apollo hurried Jennifer and themselves down the stairs and out of the townhouse. Safe in the front yard, Poppy looked up and saw smoke drifting out of the third floor. Investigating Walsh's office and bedrooms on the third floor would be postponed until the fire was out and she and Apollo were given the all clear.

It wasn't long before fire trucks, ambulances, four police officers, another set of detectives, a forensic team, and several Capulets showed up. While Poppy, Apollo, and Jennifer were being officially looked over by the EMTs, Poppy learned Apollo had heard suspicious ticking on the stairs that sounded like an old cartoon show bomb. It was unclear if they had set the bomb off or if their timing had been unlucky — or lucky, depending on how they looked at it; they could have already been up there when it went off. The bomb destroyed half of Walsh's bedroom and half of his office. One bedroom and the bathroom on that floor were untouched. There had been something worth finding up there. Now, they just had to hope the techs could piece something together.

When Poppy was finally able to slip over to check on Jennifer, she saw over Jennifer's shoulder that she was texting with a friend. Her owl eyesight easily read the messages:

Hey, it's me from yesterday. I just heard about the explosion at your uncle's. How are you doing?

Shaken. The whole place lurched.

You were THERE??

Rather than invade Jennifer's privacy more, Poppy made herself known, and Jennifer assured her that she was physically fine, if still scared. She shared that her mind kept wandering to the question: what if she'd gone up there instead of the detectives? Poppy put a comforting hand on her shoulder and told her not to think about that. Still, Jennifer's hand tightened on her phone, and she held it a little closer to her chest.

Leaving Jennifer in the care of her family, Poppy headed over to where Apollo stood; the EMTs were still looking him over. She tried not to hear the rough edge of his disoriented "Hey" that seemed to replay in her head over and over, but she wasn't particularly successful. She had no idea what he was thinking in that moment and wasn't sure she should ask; all she could think about was waking up to his smile and his deep voice.

Chapter 5

Jennifer

Finally alone and in her apartment, Jennifer leaned against the inside of her front door, trying not to freak out about her uncle's place exploding. That couldn't mean anything good.

To force her attention elsewhere, she pulled out her phone and reread her text messages. Miles had actually texted her after finding out who she was yesterday. She was sure he'd try to ignore their entire encounter. She'd always been told that Montagues were rude and callous. It was what she'd expected. Instead, he'd been concerned about her.

They'd exchanged almost a dozen quick messages before her family showed up at the scene and swarmed her. She never got to reply to his last message.

Shifting to her human form, Jennifer typed out a message letting him know she was alone and asking how he was holding up — he'd lost someone too. Bracing herself, she hit send before she could second guess her actions.

Chapter 6

Apollo

Apollo rubbed his forehead, trying to banish his headache. The day just wouldn't end.

Yesterday, interviewing all of Walsh's relatives had monopolized their time. Walsh was apparently exactly what the family expected, aside from his inclination toward water. Every theory to explain Walsh's death that the Capulets proposed involved the Montagues. These theories were all given with a superior sniff and a baleful look at Apollo. Surprisingly, Poppy hadn't tolerated anything more than a distasteful glance his way. As soon as the Capulets crossed that line, she defended him, or, more specifically, the position of detective, which included both of them.

Today was much worse in Apollo's estimation. Worse than nearly being blown up two days ago and being practically accused of colluding with murderers yesterday. Apollo shook his head at that. Before today, he would have thought that those two days would have been the worst days possible. Now, he understood why the captain had told him to avoid Poppy and hadn't bothered to tell her anything. The Capulets might have thought he and the Montagues were scum, but they did it in an aloof fashion that was all implied disdain. The Montagues weren't like that.

All day, Apollo and Poppy had been interviewing each and every Montague to see if they could get a break in the case. While they learned Lucy was into yoga and often took road trips by herself between the large work events she organized, her family dismissed that as part of her oddball, mixed-breed personality — as if that were even a thing. Most of the older set were indulgent but miffed by her. The younger Montagues were split between sharing their parents' view of Lucy and wishing they could be more freewheeling like her. None of that made the day unbearable. It was everyone's reactions to Poppy that set Apollo's whiskers in such a permanent droop that his face ached.

Nothing the Montagues actually said was incriminating, but their attitudes had Apollo questioning their innocence. It was getting harder and harder to stay objective. After the day they'd had, he could easily believe half of them would have slit Walsh's throat if given the slightest incentive. Not one of them even called him by his name; they all said "the Capulet" or "that Capulet" with derision or, in many cases, insults. Apollo had not understood that the Montagues' hate for the Capulets ran so deep.

Every single Montague that was puzzled by Lucy's life and personality had, at minimum, snarled at Poppy. Snarls, Apollo had to let go. Rude words, he had to let go, too. Lunges, whether actual or feints as some of them claimed, had Apollo physically manhandling the interviewees. He was thankful that the captain had ordered him to play up his earlier career as an athlete since it required him to stay in better shape than he might have otherwise. The Montagues, as a whole, were not on the weak side. Literally wrestling a few of them to the ground had not been the easiest thing he'd done. He was sweaty and disheveled after just the first five interviews, and they were only a quarter of the way done at most.

Apollo reminded each belligerent interviewee that attacking a police officer or detective carried serious charges. He didn't mention that it wasn't worth charging them with anything; Apollo had worked with the family long enough to know it was pointless. The family lawyer, Ms. Gue as she insisted on being called, who had followed them through the sports complex all day, would have the charges dropped in under an hour, so why bother?

Ms. Gue was the epitome of efficiency and the only hybrid in human form that they'd seen in the Montague Sports Center. She was, as always, in a nice suit and had her brown hair pulled back. Apollo knew she was the singular non-dog hybrid in the Montague family because he'd thoroughly researched the Montagues after he first met them. If he had never learned that Ms. Gue was a rabbit hybrid, he never would have guessed. She had killer instincts in the courtroom, even if her nose did start twitching in her human form after the Crisis hit.

Finding the murderer was much more important than creating mild hassles for the angrier Montagues and Ms. Gue — at least, Apollo had told himself that at the start of the day. Now, he wasn't sure. He could have given in and interviewed a few of the Montagues alone, but he wouldn't dismiss Poppy like that after she had stood up for him the day before with the Capulets.

As it was, Poppy's feathers had been plumped up in offense for hours, sticking out at odd angles from the cuffs of her brown jacket and shoved up around her face as they pushed out of the collar of her shirt. Her beige pants, which normally hung in nice lines that Apollo had noticed just that morning, were puffed out like they were filled with stuffing. Apparently, her hybrid owl legs weren't scaled as some bird hybrid's were but feathered instead.

Shaking his head, Apollo tried to stop thinking about Poppy's legs, how horrible he felt about the Montagues' treatment of her, and the way her body felt beneath him when he got his first good look at her in her human form the day before yesterday. He squeezed his eyes shut for a moment, knowing he wasn't succeeding at redirecting his thoughts. Then, he led Poppy to the office of their last interviewee — Miles Montague, the new head of marketing despite being out of college for less than two years.

Apollo opened Miles's door and saw immediately that the young man wasn't handling the loss of his aunt in stride like the rest of his family seemed to be. Miles's corgi ears were drooping, and he sat slumped in his chair. The top two buttons of his red shirt were undone, and his black tie hung loose around his neck to the point that the knot barely held together. The poor corgi hybrid was chewing on his lip and staring blankly at his cell phone which sat at the far corner of his large mahogany desk. His disheveled and depressed appearance contrasted sharply with the bright sports posters behind him. He hadn't even heard them knock.

As Apollo filled the door, a panicked expression crossed Miles's face but was quickly replaced by one of relief. When Poppy entered behind him, Miles visibly focused a little and started thinking. Still, he didn't snap or snarl at Poppy at all; that was promising. Apollo let his body relax a fraction, though he was still primed to jump between Miles and Poppy if needed.

Just as he and Poppy cleared the door, Ms. Gue pushed past them, catching Apollo off guard and causing Poppy to bump into him. The family attorney rushed over to Miles full of overt motherly concern, reminding Apollo that Miles was her nephew, though a distant one. Miles's body tensed as she hurried to him, and it was clear this was what he'd worried about when Apollo opened the door. It couldn't be denied that Miles's current appearance didn't match the unbothered image the rest of the family presented.

After she fussed over Miles like he was a pampered infant for several minutes, Miles convinced her that he'd been working through a tough marketing snafu. He was fine, and no, they didn't need to reschedule. Despite his reassurance, Ms. Gue continued to hover around him to such an extent that Miles insisted, sounding as annoyed and imperious as his father did at times, that he didn't need a lawyer present and shooed his aunt out. Displeased, she tried to dissuade him, but to no avail.

Apollo gently shut the door behind Ms. Gue, happy to not have her frowning presence for one interview. Ms. Gue knew better than to be openly aggressive toward Poppy, but she had also looked satisfied the first few times Poppy jerked back from one of the Montagues when they snapped or jumped at her. There was also that chance that she'd shoved Poppy harder than necessary to get into the room and over to Miles. After today, Ms. Gue was no longer in Apollo's good graces.

Poppy took a seat in one of the two chairs across the desk from Miles, and Apollo helped himself to the other.

"Everything alright?" Apollo asked, glancing meaningfully at the door. Miles didn't miss the implication.

"I'm—" He gestured at himself in a general fashion. "—not exactly adhering to the dress code expectations at the moment."

"Were you and your Aunt Lucy particularly close?" Poppy asked gently. Apollo noticed her feathers were a little less fluffed than before they'd entered Miles's office.

"Yeah," Miles said. His eyes darted to his phone as it lit up with a message, but he didn't reach for it. "She knew what my dad is like better than anyone, so you could say we were pretty close." Apollo didn't miss the insinuation that Miles found his dad hard to handle. More than once, Apollo had thought that Edward Montague was intense, and *he* wasn't part of the family. He didn't have constant interactions with him like Miles did.

"Had you noticed anything different about her in the last few weeks?" Apollo asked. It was a standard question they'd asked in all the interviews, but Miles was the only one to admit he was close with Lucy. Apollo hoped they might get something useful for the first time that day.

Miles reached up and scratched behind his left ear a few times. "She'd been jumpy. She used to get like that before she'd go off on one of her road trips, like she was itching to get away. But this last year, I'd noticed it more when she got back. She was always looking over her shoulder when she left the office. It was as if she thought work was chasing after her. I asked her a few times if she was okay, and she patted me on the head like she's done since I can remember. She seemed even more on edge this last month. I should've pushed her about it." His eyes darted to his phone as it lit up again.

"Do you know where she'd go on her road trips?" Apollo had found that no one had a clue where the black sheep of the family went, and they didn't care either.

"I wouldn't until she came back. She kept a photo album that she showed me after each trip. She always went somewhere different."

"Did she just start sharing the album with you this past year?" Apollo asked.

Poppy clarified, "The same past year that she was a little jumpy about work?"

"I hadn't made that connection, but yeah. The timeline matches," Miles said. "I assumed she was sharing it because I was permanently back in the area after college and asked about her trips." Quietly, Miles admitted, "I doubt anyone else genuinely asked her about where she went." He cleared his throat and continued, "She wouldn't tell me the names of the places; she'd just show me the photos and say what she liked about it there. If it was a recognizable attraction or a well-known place, she'd wink at me like it was our secret."

"What did she like about the places?" Poppy asked.

Miles's eyes drifted off to the side before he muttered, "That they weren't here," so quietly that Apollo barely caught what he said. Looking back at Apollo and Poppy, Miles said, "All the places were beautiful and new to her. Aunt Lucy liked changing things up." Apollo was sure both of Miles's statements were the truth, but the latter sounded more like something Lucy would say, even if she meant the former.

"Is there any chance her change in behavior could have started while you were off at college?" Apollo said.

"No," Miles said with conviction. He hadn't paused to think about it. "I noticed it about six months after I started working here. It could have been happening a month or maybe three before that if it wasn't as pronounced, but no earlier."

"Any changes in her work here or her life outside of work that you think could be connected to her jumpiness?"

"Not that I know of. Like I said, she'd just pat me on the head if I asked."

Apollo noted this information down. It was more to go on than they had before. They'd need to track down the photo album in her condo. Maybe go visit the places she went, assuming they could identify them and that they were close enough. They'd at least send her photo to the police departments near the attractions and have them ask around to see if there was any connection between the trips and her and Walsh's deaths. If they were lucky, she would have left financial footprints to follow too.

"Do you have any thoughts about your aunt being found with Walsh Capulet?" Poppy asked. Apollo tensed for a second. In all the other interviews, he'd asked that question, and then the aggression toward Poppy ratcheted up several notches as if she were a Capulet herself. It was generally at this question that he had to physically restrain the interviewee.

Miles looked at Poppy and shook his head before his eyes darted to his phone nervously. After a moment of silence, he focused back on Poppy.

"I hate to say it," Miles said, swallowing hard, "but their deaths have to be connected to why Walsh Capulet's place blew up, right?"

Apollo and Poppy exchanged looks; Miles had acknowledged Walsh by his first name. He sounded more worried than accusatory, too. Yes, he had laid some of the blame on the Capulet victim, but he didn't look happy about it. And, technically, Miles hadn't actually blamed the cat. He'd pointed out that the two events had to be connected, which was not a large leap; they were taking the likelihood very seriously.

To be safe, a bomb squad had checked Lucy's condo and a different pair of detectives had searched it the day before to give Poppy and Apollo more time to recover from the explosion. They'd found nothing out of the ordinary and definitely no bombs. But the bomb at Walsh's place had to be connected to at least his death if not to both his and Lucy's. It seemed improbable Lucy was in the wrong place at the wrong time, especially since the thumps from Felix's Corner's recordings hinted that Lucy died first.

Apollo let himself fully relax in his chair for the first time since they had arrived at Montague Legacy Sports. "We're investigating that possibility," Apollo told Miles. Miles nodded, adjusted his position in his seat a little, and glanced again at his phone. "Do you need to check your phone?"

Mile's wide eyes looked up at Apollo with another flash of panic like the one Apollo had seen when they'd opened the door to his office. "I'm sure it can wait," he said with a forced casualness. "If someone needs to contact me, they'll call my office phone." He nodded at the landline sitting on his desk.

While Miles was likely doing something he shouldn't be, it didn't feel connected to Lucy and Walsh's deaths. It struck Apollo as something that Miles didn't want his family to pester him about — like with how he wasn't adhering to the dress code today. Still, Apollo would keep it in mind moving forward on the off chance it factored into the case somehow.

After a few more quick questions, Apollo left his card with Miles and told him to call if he thought of anything else about his aunt. It was important that Miles's interview didn't appear any longer than anyone else's, especially since Miles had sent the family lawyer out *and* given them useful information.

A frustrated Ms. Gue was waiting for them outside of Miles's office and escorted Poppy and Apollo out of Montague Legacy Sports under the watchful glares of every Montague they passed. Apollo found it difficult not to wrap his arm around Poppy and try to shield her from the open hostility, but he knew he couldn't do that and keep the Montagues' trust. He didn't think Poppy would want him to do it either; they didn't have that type of relationship.

Once they were back in his car and several blocks away from Montague Stadium, Apollo gave himself a full body shake as he shifted from his hybrid mouse form and into his human skin. In unspoken accord, Poppy shifted too. Her dark brown pixie haircut stuck out at awkward angles that did eye-catching things to her lighter highlights. It reminded Apollo of her ruffled feathers from the interviews and made him more annoyed with the Montagues. Other than her hair, Poppy looked as put together and enticing as usual.

In the small space of his car, her pine needle scent made it impossible not to think about her. Apollo found himself wondering if she wore eyeliner or if the delicate, dark edges of her eyes were carried over from her hybrid owl form, sort of like the color of his hair. He'd finally seen her eyes up close after the explosion when he was lying on top of her and hadn't been able to shake the question.

"I always feel the need to spend time in my human form after being there," Apollo explained. It rubbed him the wrong way that the only humans there were just that — humans. Not a single hybrid was in their human form — with the exception of Ms. Gue. Such conformity to a preferred form, regardless of the direction it took, felt unnatural.

Poppy snorted. "They do seem like a friendly bunch."

"They're not normally that bad." Apollo's voice trailed off. He'd thought the Montagues were more of the fun-loving sports types if arrogant, but after today, they obviously could embody the worst sports-associated behaviors too.

"Unless you're a Capulet or connected to a Capulet in any way, right?"

"Apparently." He didn't bother hiding his disgust from Poppy. He'd known that the Montagues didn't like the Capulets, but this was his first time working a case that involved the Capulets. Evidently, that meant he had to throw out all of his prior knowledge of the family; he never would have thought they could be this bad.

Poppy's hand touched the back of his on the stick shift for a brief moment. He knew she was trying to tell him it wasn't his fault they were like that, but his body told him she was reaching out for other reasons.

"Did anyone set off your instincts? You know them better." Her voice was normal and business-like, forcing him to push down his non-work-appropriate urge to be a little more personal with Poppy.

Apollo thought through the different interviews they'd had that day. It was convenient that the Montagues employed their whole family down to the teenagers who were picking up a few part-time hours. In one day, they'd been able to interview everyone old enough to have unsupervised time.

"Edward knew something he wasn't sharing," Apollo said after a moment. "It could be something irrelevant that he doesn't want throwing a pall on his sister after her death, but I'm not sure."

"I noticed that too," Poppy said. "I thought Lucy's assistant's assistant was a little questionable."

With Miles's comment that Lucy acted like *work* was following her, Apollo thought it might be worth it to pull that particular Montague Legacy Sports employee in for more questioning; he was "family" but oddly didn't have an influential position. "That's a good point. We'll talk with him more. Also, Miles was keeping something close to the vest, but I'm not sure it has anything to do with our investigation," he added.

Poppy tilted her head back and forth, considering what he said.

"Do you want to mull over everything at my place?" Apollo asked suddenly. He made a point of not looking at Poppy. He couldn't believe he'd just suggested that. Before she could read anything into his invitation, he added, "That way, we don't have to snipe at each other like we'd need to do in the office with an audience."

"You might lose an ear if I have to deal with any more aggravation today," Poppy muttered.

"An ear? Why an ear?"

"Seems like the easiest part of you to tear off."

Apollo glanced over at Poppy and raised his eyebrows. "You've given this some thought."

"A jury would agree I was provoked," she said with a shrug.

Apollo chuckled and drove them to his place. He liked the idea of her taking a bite out of him. He liked it a little too much.

Chapter 7

Miles

Miles carefully listened to the detectives' and Aunt Gue's footsteps get quieter and quieter. When he couldn't hear them anymore, he lunged for his phone. He knew exactly who both text messages were from.

Are we still doing this?

I'll be waiting where we first met.

He didn't care that he was a complete mess. He was going to meet her. Last night, she'd told him not to beat himself up about not pushing his aunt to tell him what was bothering her. Jenny hadn't realized that her uncle was in trouble either, and she spent at least thirty hours a week around him.

Miles quickly typed out a message, saying he'd be a few minutes late, but he'd be there. He fixed his tie in preparation for walking through the office, picked up his briefcase that held a different shirt and a jacket for him to change into, and left for what his calendar said was "a meeting."

Chapter 8

Poppy

Poppy took in Apollo's house as he pulled into his driveway, feeling more self-conscious than she probably should. She split her attention between taking a good look at where he lived and trying to not think about him. It wasn't easy. Her awareness of Apollo had been kicked into overdrive after seeing him physically wrestle the Montagues into submission; who knew a mouse hybrid grappling with, and besting, dog hybrids would be that captivating? It would be an understatement to say that his efficiency in subduing a number of former professional athletes had impressed her. That he was now in his human form sitting next to her didn't help her focus. She felt as if she could sense his every movement beside her. Luckily, she couldn't easily ignore his house either.

The off-white home had a small yard out front that had been mowed recently, but that was where the normalcy ended. His front door was arched and honestly looked like a cartoon mouse hole-in-the-wall. The windows were all round, with trim dividing each pane into four sections. Two of the windows were big, but five were small. She wanted to tease him and ask if she'd have to find her way through a maze inside, but she thought that might be overstepping. The house looked like it had been constructed pre-Crisis, but it was so hybrid specific, she wondered if the aged look was an affectation.

Next to her, Apollo put the car in park and twisted around to grab the case file from the backseat. By the time he'd twisted back, she'd stopped studying his house and was looking at him. Poppy knew his police-siren-red shirt was a blending tactic. Seventy-five percent of the employees at Montague Legacy Sports wore red that day. The percentage skyrocketed if you only considered the family members. The bright shade of his shirt made his gray hair look darker than normal.

"Let's head in," he said. Poppy let herself out of the car and shut the door as Apollo rounded the hood and waved her behind him toward the front door. He seemed in a hurry, and she wondered if it had anything to do with not being seen together by the Montagues. That was a little paranoid in her estimation, but then again, Captain Starl didn't want them to seem friendly, and being at Apollo's house absolutely crossed that line.

Standing behind him, Poppy marveled at his towering front door. It hadn't appeared quite so large from the car. Poppy found it odd that the lock and handle were in the middle. Once Apollo had it unlocked, he pushed the right half's bottom three-fourths into the house, revealing a typical rectangular doorway. The left half of the door and the arch above weren't real. That was different. Poppy followed Apollo in and across the threshold without comment and looked around, not hiding her interest.

The living room that opened up in front of her and to the right had beige carpet and cream walls. Apollo had three mismatched armchairs partially circling a free-standing wood fireplace. Each armchair had a different shape and was a slightly different shade of green. To complete the circle, a burnt orange, futon-looking couch lay directly on the ground accompanied by dark brown pillows. The seating ensemble was both eclectic and oddly homey. Between the seating and fireplace was a butcher block coffee table. The glow from the living room lights revealed a shadowy kitchen to the left of the entry. A dark hallway extended deeper into the house. Every passageway she could see was rounded into arches. Real arches.

"A big fan of the mouse hole arch?" she finally asked, unable to keep her laughter from her voice.

"Uh, no," Apollo said. He slipped his shoes off, and Poppy followed suit. "I went out of town for a few months, back when I was working that rhino hybrid case." Poppy remembered hearing about that. Before the Crisis, the man had just finished bottle-raising a rhino, but the rhino still had an imprint on the man and was mature enough to sacrifice himself to save the person who had raised him. He was the only rhino hybrid in existence as far as anyone knew.

"Well, my brother Orion decided to *mousify* my house as a joke while I was gone. He works in construction. It was child's play for him. I'm not opposed to the arches and mock tunnel aspect, but..." He shrugged as if he couldn't do anything about it. Poppy physically felt his hapless shrug since he was standing at least as close to her as he had at the crime scene when she'd looked out the window. She took a breath and focused on the conversation and not on remembering how rough his voice had sounded after the explosion.

"Orion? Your brother is named Orion?"

Apollo grimaced and stepped away from her and into the living room. "Yeah. Our dad is really into mythology. Apparently, the first time I saw my little brother, I tried to bite him." Poppy widened her eyes at that comment and sat in the grass-green, rounded back armchair he gestured at for her. "In my defense, I was barely two. Still, our dad thought it was funny."

"He named your brother after someone you tricked your mythological twin sister into killing?" Poppy clarified. She ran an admiring hand along the armrest as the plush velvet of her chair registered. It was soft, and the cushions had the right amount of give to wrap her up but not let her sink in and feel smothered.

"Basically, but alas, no sister to do the deed," he joked.

Poppy almost asked if Orion was a mouse hybrid too, but she didn't. It was rude to ask people about the hybrid makeup of their family. One never knew what dynamics were going on behind the scenes. Plus, when the Crisis hit, Apollo wouldn't necessarily have had the same pets as the rest of his family or have been living with them. She didn't know if he was already at the police academy or finishing up college then. Poppy, herself, had been in college and volunteering at a wildlife rescue, nursing an owl back to health. No one else in her family was a bird hybrid; there was no reason for Orion to be a rodent hybrid like Apollo. He might be completely human if he hadn't had a pet when the Crisis hit for all she knew.

Apollo rested his hands on the back of the hunter-green armchair and asked her what she wanted to drink. Poppy covertly watched him walk away as she tried to decide if her sense that he was delicious came from the fact that he was a mouse hybrid or the way he moved. She was leaning less and less toward the former now that she knew, from his broad shoulders down to his narrow hips, that he was solid muscle. He was a smidge wiry for his frame, but very strong as he'd proven throughout the day. Poppy felt the urge to fan herself. Rather than being caught checking him out, she leaned forward and flipped open the file on the coffee table while Apollo brought back two cicada ciders from the fridge.

After passing her a cider, he crouched down in front of the fireplace and set a few logs ablaze. The crackle of flames and the creaking of what Poppy suspected were cedar logs increased as the fire took hold. Then, Apollo settled into the high back hunter-green chair beside her and directly across from the fire. She wondered if this was what he did every evening, or if he lit the fire for her. Shaking her head at the foolish thought, Poppy reached for the top page of the file.

"So," Apollo said, "any—"

The sound of his front door opening cut him off, and Poppy snapped her head to the left to see who was coming in and closed the file she'd opened.

"Hey!" a man's voice called out. "Since Carly is out of town, I thought I'd come over and see how bickering with the pretty detective went today."

Poppy felt her cheeks warm and saw Apollo look at the ceiling as if in pain. The man rounded the door and froze halfway through the process of kicking off his tennis shoes. He looked a lot like Apollo but a little taller and softer, more snuggly. He wore a dark sweatshirt and jeans. Unlike Apollo's mouse gray hair, he had black hair. In his hand, he carried a charcuterie board piled high with meats and cheeses.

"Uh," he said.

"Poppy, meet my brother Orion," Apollo said, still looking up at the ceiling, which made Poppy smirk a little at him. "Orion, this is Poppy or Detective Barrdom."

Orion unfroze, kicked off his second shoe, and gave an apologetic, "Hiya Poppy." Then, to the back of the chair his brother sat in, he said as if coaxing a cranky critter out with bribery, "I brought foo-ood."

Apollo sighed loudly, and Orion clearly took that to mean he was welcome. He came over and set the charcuterie board on the coffee table on top of the corner of their police file, bringing a faint smell of sawdust with him.

"Ooh, they had the ciders in stock." He hurried into the kitchen to grab his own cicada cider. As he turned away, Poppy didn't see anything built into his clothes that would indicate he was a hybrid with a tail like Apollo, but that didn't mean he was human either. When Orion came back, he plopped down on the odd futon, finally looking at his brother for the first time. "Wow, that shirt... Did a Christmas tree vomit you out?" Poppy tried to suppress her laugh at the accurate color assessment of the siren red shirt against the hunter green chair.

"How long is Carly gone for again?" Apollo asked, completely refusing to acknowledge his brother's comment. Glancing at Poppy and seeing that she was trying, and failing, to not laugh, he added, "Carly's his wife." She'd assumed as much and, with a nod, tamped down harder on her laughter. She had mild success.

"All week," Orion said dejectedly. "She won't get back until Saturday." He took a sip of his cider. "But enough about me. Poppy," he smiled at her, and she could swear she saw an evil glint in his eye, "how's working with my big bro?"

Poppy saw Apollo freeze for a split second as he reached for a piece of white cheese, but then he kept moving as if nothing was amiss. She wasn't fooled. Obviously, he'd talked to his brother about her *and* commented that he thought she was pretty. Apparently, the attraction wasn't one-sided.

"Interesting," Poppy said, putting on her most innocent, wide-eyed, owlish look. "Never thought I'd see a mouse hybrid wrestle a rabid dog hybrid to the ground and twist his arm behind his back."

Orion blinked several times before looking between the two of them and asking, "What?"

Poppy let Apollo fill his brother in about how their day had gone. She could have sworn Apollo forgot she was there as he worked himself up into ranting about how ridiculous the "victim's family" had behaved that day and how angry he was about the whole thing. Orion's eyes flicked to Poppy a few times during Apollo's tirade, and she shrugged at him. Apollo didn't cross the line and reveal case details, but he was clearly comfortable sharing his emotions with his brother — more comfortable than most men. She had no idea that the Montagues' behavior had gotten to Apollo that badly. He seemed more upset about it than she was, and she'd been pretty upset about it earlier.

"Well, I'm, uh, glad you're okay, Poppy," Orion said when Apollo finally trailed off.

Apollo's eyes darted to her, and his mouth hung slightly ajar. He snapped it shut after a second; he *had* forgotten she was there for a moment while he went off about how sickening it was to have to put up with how the Montagues treated her. He obviously hadn't meant to say all of that in front of her, at least not in that way.

"Yup. No worse for wear," Poppy muttered before taking another sip of her cider to wash down the salty prosciutto she'd been distractedly nibbling on the last ten minutes while Apollo vented. She desperately searched for a way to defuse the blush she knew was going to show up if she thought much more about Apollo's anger on her behalf. She was really starting to like him, and not just because he looked delicious. She grabbed on to what she was sure was an annoyingly common joke, but at least it was something.

"Anyway, Apollo tells me he's going to trick someone into killing you."

"Ah yes," Orion replied seriously. "He always has something afoot, but I'm too lovable and no one can go through with it."

"I see," Poppy pretended to look at Orion suspiciously until both brothers started chuckling.

"Okay, okay," Apollo said.

He then turned the conversation on to other casual topics, but they got no work done by the time Poppy called it a night. Apollo drove her back to the station for her car and shared more stories about him and his brother along the way. When he pulled in next to her car and looked over at her, Poppy could have sworn her heart stopped beating.

Apollo wasn't looking at her like a fellow detective. He was just looking at her like she was pretty and like he wanted to spend more time with her. A lot of time. His gaze drifted down to her mouth, and Poppy felt herself lean minutely towards him.

"I'll see you in the morning?" she whispered. His eyes flew back up to hers, and he nodded. He had that *deer-in-the-headlights* look again. Poppy gave him a small smile and climbed out before she did something stupid, like lean across the car console and kiss him.

Safely in her car, she steadied herself. Disappointment coursed through her. It sucked that nothing could come of their mutual attraction. The whole Capulet and Montague thing had long fingers.

Chapter 9

Apollo

"**M**onkshood?" Apollo repeated back to Mallary Hasli, the forensic tech for their case.

He forced himself not to glance at Poppy standing beside him. They were both in their hybrid forms; Apollo assumed now that Poppy was just comfortable in her owl form since the captain probably hadn't advised her to be in hybrid form as much as possible to cater to the Capulets' preferences. He apparently hadn't advised her about much of anything when it came to dealing with the Capulets as far as Apollo could tell. Or maybe she could see more in her owl form; her eyes were larger than in her human form. Or maybe he was paying too much attention to what she looked like and how pretty he found her. Regardless of why he was noticing her eyes, asking people about why they choose a certain form was considered an extremely personal question; it would be inappropriate for him to ask her after having spoken to her for the first time not four full days earlier.

"Lucy Montague was poisoned with monkshood?" Poppy asked.

"Yes," Mallary confirmed. She tucked a stray piece of blonde hair behind her ear that the lab air conditioning had blown into her face. The constant hum of machines almost drowned out the air conditioner that was, as always, set much too cold for Apollo's comfort. Every forensics lab Apollo had ever been in had been freezing; it was something about ideal running temperatures for electronics.

"But it wasn't in her tea?" Poppy clarified.

"It wasn't in the teapot on her table nor in her cup of tea, but there was some mixed with the tea in her stomach," Mallary said. Apollo looked at the three monitors Mallary had all the case details up on and was happy he didn't have to juggle different screens at his desk.

"And we're sure that those were the teapot and teacup she used?" Apollo wracked his brain for an explanation of how Lucy was given the poison.

"The fingerprints on the teapot and cup are numerous and all in natural places. It would be extremely unlikely that someone replaced the teapot and cup after she died and tried to make it look like it was the one she used." Mallary pulled up an enhanced photo of the sheer number of Lucy's prints on both items. Apollo would have guessed, even without Miles's tip, that something was bothering Lucy before her death. She'd never struck him as a fidgeter, and that many different prints belied serious fidgeting.

"The lipstick marks on the cup match what the victim was wearing when she died. The saliva is hers as well." Mallary added while indicating two matching bar graphs that confirmed the lipstick was not only the same type, but from the same manufacturing batch.

"In what time frame can we assume she was poisoned?" Poppy asked.

"Depending on the dose, monkshood can start working in as little as ten minutes, but it can take several hours to do its job. Given the amount in her system and sitting unprocessed in her stomach, her symptoms would have started closer to the ten-minute mark." Mallary pointed at a chart on the screen farthest to the left that had milliliters of poison to pounds of the consumer diagrammed. "I've estimated her time of death to be between twelve and one, so—"

"Twelve and one?" Apollo asked.

"That can't be right," Poppy said. "The tea cottage owner found her and Walsh dead at 11:37." In order to look at the chart, she moved close enough to him that he caught a whiff of the perfume she wore. It was the same as the last two days — pine needles. He was really starting to like pine needles, but the fact that he could smell it meant she was standing too close to him. Particularly since they weren't alone. While he should have moved away from her, he couldn't bring himself to do it just yet.

"Even if they checked for a pulse," Mallary said, "they might not have felt one. A weakened pulse is one of the symptoms."

"She might have still been alive when Officers Kent and Cane arrived on the scene just after noon?" Apollo felt his stomach clench. Poppy's feathered pinky brushed the back of his hand as if trying to comfort him, but he was too appalled at the moment to make her back off. He appreciated the comfort the small touch gave him.

"It's probable, but if she ingested the monkshood between 10:30 and 11:30, she would have been too far gone to save," Mallary said. She'd gotten back to Poppy's original question, but Apollo remained stuck on the fact that Lucy had still been alive when she was found.

"It's possible Walsh wasn't present when she was poisoned," Poppy said aloud, working through the timeline.

Focusing on the facts, Apollo pushed away his horror. "The Capulet wasn't poisoned..." Apollo let his voice trail off with derision to give the implication he thought Walsh was both the perpetrator and not worthy of having a first name — like the Montagues had done the day before.

"It was in his system, but in an amount that could have been from prolonged contact since the deadliest effects do come from ingestion," Mallary allowed. She didn't appear sold on the idea, but Apollo grabbed onto it as an avenue that needed to be explored.

"We already know that the Capulet died between eleven and twelve, so he had to be present when she was poisoned," Apollo pushed.

Poppy pulled away from him and argued, "He could have entered after she ingested the poison and interrupted her murder. It would explain why his time of death is earlier."

"But that doesn't account for him having *trace* amounts of the poison," Apollo challenged, trying to make it sound like Walsh had even less poison in his system.

In any other circumstance, this would have been a calm exchange of ideas and theories, but with him pretending to disdain Poppy, it seemed she couldn't help but be rude right back to him. If he constantly proffered close-minded views that made the Capulets look guilty, she, in turn, countered with reasonable points everyone would side with.

And, for now, he'd rather focus on being rude to her for show than on the possibility that Lucy might have been alive when he had arrived. If the dispatcher had sent medics instead of officers, would it have changed anything?

Facts, motives, timelines, and aggravating Poppy when they were around others, and trying not to kiss her when they were alone — that was what he needed to give his attention to. Not what-ifs.

It was likely that Walsh was the shout and large thud on the video recording at 11:21. He could have died a full hour before Lucy fully succumbed to the poison. That said, Walsh might have been there when Lucy was poisoned or poisoned her himself.

In either case, it was unlikely that Lucy murdered Walsh. She couldn't have overpowered him and slit his throat without getting blood on herself after being poisoned. She probably couldn't do it in perfect health. While Lucy was athletic, Apollo knew she did yoga-style activities, not martial arts. And the positioning of her body suggested that Lucy fell out of her chair. Why would she sit down in the chair after murdering Walsh? It made more sense if the earlier, medium-sized thud was Lucy falling out of her chair due to the poison.

Regardless of if Walsh had something to do with Lucy's poisoning, his murderer, if not *their* murderer, was unaccounted for.

"What's the difference in monkshood toxicity between cat and dog hybrids?" Poppy asked in a tone that, to an outside observer, sounded annoyed with Apollo's very presence, but was more professional than it had been a second ago when directed at him.

"Thank you, Detective Barrdom; that's an insightful question." Apollo held in a snort at Mallary's tone; it said he was being an ass. Which he already knew. "It hasn't been thoroughly investigated in hybrids as no one wants to volunteer for experimentation, for obvious reasons. I, however, theorize that it's deadlier for canine hybrids since it is also known as wolfsbane."

"If they were both poisoned with equal quantities, Miss Montague would have had a more severe and instantaneous reaction?" Poppy said.

"Yes," Mallary said firmly. "Even if it is equally toxic to both types of hybrids, her lower body mass alone would indicate a quicker and more severe reaction to the poison."

"And what would she have experienced?" Apollo asked. He made sure to cross his arms like he resented Poppy's line of questioning.

Mallary gave Apollo a look as if imploring him to be the professional she knew him to be. "There would have been a tingling sensation, numbness, possibly the feeling of ice in her veins to start. The real issue comes as the lungs and respiratory system freeze and breathing becomes near impossible until eventual suffocation."

"Was she conscious throughout all of that?" Poppy asked with the same concern Apollo had seen her extend for anyone suffering, regardless of who they were.

A grimace crossed Mallary's face as she waggled her head back and forth in a way that reminded Apollo that, despite Mallary being a goat hybrid, she spent considerable time with her best friend, who was a chicken hybrid. "It's possible."

Not wanting to dwell on what Lucy might have endured, Apollo pushed on: "And what of the knife and wound on the Capulet?"

"I recovered one set of partial prints on the knife. Between the blood and ridges on the handle, I couldn't identify any others. The set I found matches Walsh Capulet," Mallary said. "This information would lend itself to a suicide, especially given the positioning of the knife in relation to the body on the ground. However, there should have been more blood pooled around the body. The wound looks like it was inflicted near the time of death but post-mortem, negating the suicide theory."

"Have you found anything that explains his death beyond some Monkshood in his system?" Poppy asked.

Mallary shook her head.

"His cause of death might be obscured by the knife wound," Apollo said, thinking aloud. "We can ask the medical examiner to take a closer look at his neck." Poppy and Mallary made noises of agreement, and Apollo tried to think of something snarky to add to keep up his argumentative front.

"Add in the explosion at his townhouse, and without a doubt, we're looking at a third party," Poppy mused aloud before he came up with something.

"Anything from the explosion?" Apollo rubbed his neck where it was a little stiff from being flung around by the blast three days prior. Wrestling with a couple of the stronger Montagues yesterday had not helped his recovery. His mind kept turning on Walsh's slit throat while Mallary answered.

"Nothing telling yet. The bomb was basic. Homemade with things anyone could get. A simple internet search would produce several sets of instructions." Mallary passed them a list of bomb parts that anyone could get their hands on. "The blast itself was only as big as it was because a small propane tank, like for camping, sat next to it. No prints on anything yet, but some parts are still being processed. I'm not finished resuscitating the papers that were partially burned in the ensuing fire."

"What about the knife? Anything unique about it I should take into account?" Apollo asked, purposefully leaving Poppy out of his question to maintain his charade.

Mallary looked down her nose at him. "Yes. It's not what I would think anyone would pick for a quick in and out murder, but it was plenty sharp even if the victim's neck wasn't slit very deep."

"What makes it a poor choice of murder weapon?" Poppy asked. Apollo admired how her professionalism and focus seemed to dismiss him without her doing a thing. She was better at their bickering than he was.

"The etching on the blade is nearly impossible to clean completely. An expert would have trouble erasing all traces of a victim's blood. Also, it's a puukko knife, reminiscent of the knives you see in numerous tourist shops by West Pukanto if the etching is any indication. I would think that, if you had a suspect, someone there might remember who purchased it if it was bought in the past year. It's high quality. The type of high quality that comes with a hefty price tag, but is still often bought as a fancy souvenir."

Apollo wrote West Pukanto in his notebook. He and Poppy would need to look into that place more once they had a suspect.

"Thanks, Mallary. Keep *both of us* updated if you find anything more," Poppy said.

Keeping the ruse up as they left, Apollo watched Poppy turn away from Mallary under the excuse of glowering at her. Poppy flicked a hand out toward the door in an after-you gesture that would have been courteous if her movements weren't so sharp and irritated.

Alone in the hallway, Apollo whispered, "You think they were both poisoned?"

"It's more plausible than Walsh poisoning Lucy and then another person coming in and murdering just him," she whispered back. Apollo silently loved how close Poppy stood to him and breathed in her pine needle perfume. She was completely oblivious to the effect she had on him. "Poisoning someone doesn't fit his personality. He was adamant about protecting his employees. I can't see him actively trying to harm someone. And if the murderer used too much on Lucy and not enough on Walsh, then he'd need to resort to cutting Walsh's throat. If Walsh was half-dead from the poison when his throat was slit, then there'd be less blood pumping through his system from what Mallary said about monkshood."

"But that doesn't explain why they were together or why they were targeted," Apollo muttered back. Before they exited the hallway and entered the main floor of desks, he made sure to take a big step away from Poppy.

From the right, Apollo heard someone call out his and Poppy's names above the general noise of their fellow detectives and officers working in the large room. He turned his head and saw Officer Kent waving them over.

"I've got Burney Oliver and his lawyer waiting for you in interrogation room D," Kent said, talking about the assistant to Lucy's assistant. "He is shifty, even for an Italian greyhound hybrid." Apollo suppressed his disappointment that Burney had had the forethought to bring Ms. Gue with him.

"Right," Apollo answered, ignoring the jibe at Italian greyhound hybrids. Something about their skinniness and bulgy eyes wigged most people out. "That's great, Kent. I'll be right over to talk to him."

"*We*'ll be right over to talk to him," Poppy snapped at the back of Apollo's head. It took everything he had not to smile when her beak clicked shut in an angry snap, a smidge closer to his ear than was probably called for. He would have had more fun getting to irritate Poppy the last few years than avoiding her; granted, it was only fun now because they both knew it was an act.

As they passed by Poppy's desk, he paused while she flipped through three folders that had been dropped off while they talked with Mallary. Finding whatever she had been looking for, Poppy shoved one of the folders into his chest with enough force that, caught off guard, Apollo was knocked back a step. His mind flashed to other scenarios where he'd be very down to have Poppy shove him back a step before he could stop it. To cover for his racing mind, he flipped the folder open.

There were six photos inside. Two of the photos were recent shots of both Lucy and Walsh in their hybrid forms. The other four were of them in their human forms. They each had a headshot that was as respectable as possible of their corpses. Then, there were pictures of each of them pre-Crisis when they didn't have hybrid forms yet. As Poppy had said the first day, Walsh hadn't changed much; though his hair had become lighter with white hair interspersed throughout. Lucy's photos, however, didn't even look like the same person. Ten years ago, her hair hadn't been long and black, but had been styled into a hot pink and light blue pixie cut.

Her makeup was also different to the point that it was hard to tell that the two photos were of the same person.

Apollo looked up from the folder, but Poppy was no longer at her desk. He glanced around and saw her rounding the corner to the interrogation rooms. He scurried after her, trying to suppress his bewilderment and project annoyance instead. Apollo seriously doubted he managed it if the half-suppressed chuckles of their coworkers were anything to go by.

He caught up with Poppy as she reached interrogation room D. Putting his hand on the door before she had the chance to pull it open, he forced her to stop for a second.

"Plan first," Apollo spit out.

"Enemy cop," she said, pointing at herself. "Ally cop." Her index finger flicked his chest. Apollo ignored the spark that shot through him at the contact.

"How about interested but firm cop," he pointed at himself, "and bored cop who has better things to do," he finished, pointing at her.

"Isn't that what I said?" Poppy sighed. "It's how he'll see it anyway."

"Fair enough," Apollo muttered. She was right. Burney hadn't appreciated Poppy being in the Montague offices for the interviews; he was as rude to her as the rest of the family had been, but he hadn't tried to attack her. It was appalling that not attacking Poppy was a point in his favor.

Apollo opened the door and walked in first. Both Burney and Ms. Gue looked up when he entered, and he watched Burney sneer at Poppy as she followed him in. Ms. Gue's eyes narrowed a little, but otherwise she didn't object to Poppy's presence.

Burney was, as Apollo expected him to be, in his Italian greyhound hybrid form. His glare peeked out from under his white fedora hat, and his ears were pinned back in dislike. The skinny black scarf around his neck seemed to replace a tie that would never work with the Montague red sweater he was wearing. His cologne overpowered the small room with a musky odor that reminded Apollo of his grandfather. Behind him, Apollo heard Poppy push a puff of air out her beak in response to the smell overload.

Ms. Gue wore a black suit with a red pocket square to remind everyone of her allegiance to the family despite shunning her hybrid form. Her light brown hair was pulled back into a low ponytail and her nose had already twitched twice. Not for the first time, Apollo wondered what she'd been doing around a rabbit during the Crisis.

"Ms. Gue, Burney, thank you for coming in today." In a dismissive voice, Apollo added, "You remember Detective Barrdom from yesterday, yes? Great." He moved on as if Poppy only deserved that much acknowledgement. Sighing, Poppy leaned against the wall beside the viewing glass. Taking a seat in one of the chairs across the table from Burney and Ms. Gue, Apollo asked. "Burney, could you remind me how you're connected to the Montagues? There's a familial connection somewhere, isn't there?"

"Pamela Montague is the sister-in-law of my cousin," Burney shared as if the connection were a great honor.

"Pamela is a golden retriever hybrid who married Edward and Lucy Montague's cousin Harry, right?"

"That's correct," Ms. Gue confirmed. If Apollo remembered correctly, Ms. Gue's connection to the Montagues also came through cousin Harry Montague's extended branch of the family in some convoluted way.

As Ms. Gue finished speaking, a yip came from Burney's briefcase. Then, the head of an actual Italian greyhound, wearing a scarf and sweater that matched Burney's, popped out. Burney leaned down and picked up his dog as if bringing a pet was expected in an interrogation room.

Apollo assumed it was a show dog. He hadn't been big on dog shows pre-Crisis, but post-Crisis, Apollo found the idea more and more odd. Often, the handler was the same breed as the dog they were showing, but not always. There were the occasional other non-dog hybrids and a handful of humans showing dogs. It wasn't his scene.

"When did you start working at Montague Legacy Sports?" Poppy asked Burney from her place behind Apollo's right shoulder. He imagined her examining her talons for chips or something while she spoke.

"I have been working there for a decade," Burney said importantly.

"In the family events planning department?" Apollo asked.

"I was transferred over there two years ago."

"Did Lucy request you, or did you ask for the transfer?" Apollo inquired, hoping for a reaction at the mention of Lucy. Ms. Gue's eyes narrowed at the question, but she didn't say anything. Yet.

Burney's lip curled for a second before he suppressed his reaction by coddling his dog. "Edward shifted me over since the area needed more help. He knows I do what I can for the family." Burney obviously didn't think much of Lucy. Maybe even looked down on her.

Edward though? That was interesting. Apollo took a leap and connected the tenuous dots: "He's the one who told you to follow Lucy around town?" Apollo asked as if he were confirming facts that were common knowledge.

Burney froze in mid-pet of his dog. His big eyes were wide and extra bulgy. Ms. Gue sat as still as a statue. Burney was the only person who struck Apollo as being willing to stalk Lucy and think it an honor to assist the family. And Edward had been hiding something. This would explain a lot if it were true.

"You're the one who found out Lucy and the Capulet were dead," Apollo continued as if Burney had acknowledged the last statement as correct. "You let Edward know his sister was dead and a Capulet was involved. Do I have that right?" Apollo glanced down at his notepad as if these facts were all in his notebook from the interviews. He was pretty sure Burney wasn't even on Kent and Cane's list of family members who arrived on scene at Felix's Corner.

Ms. Gue glanced at Burney as if she was trying to assess him and replan her strategy. Burney cleared his throat and raised his nose a hair, suddenly looking even haughtier than before.

"I need a mom—" Ms. Gue started.

Burney spoke over her: "When Lucy started ducking into dark corners and shifting to her human form like she didn't want to be seen, we thought it was prudent to check up on her. You know, make sure she wasn't putting herself in dangerous situations." Ms. Gue's nose and top lip twitched like she wanted to curl her mouth into a disgusted snarl. Burney wasn't a great client.

"Of course," Apollo said as if Burney's explanation made complete sense, which it didn't.

"I need a moment with my client," Ms. Gue cut in quickly before Burney could divulge more. Her veneer of professionalism had returned. Apollo followed Poppy out of the room while Ms. Gue and Burney conferred.

"Well done," Poppy murmured.

Apollo couldn't help the warm feeling that coursed through him at her compliment, but an officer walked by them in the hallway, so Apollo arrogantly said, "Did you doubt me?" instead of "Thanks."

Poppy's response left her complimentary tone far behind in the dust when she said, "I told you it had to be a Montague who ID'd Lucy in her human form."

Apollo ducked his head to hide his smile at the attitude she'd laced into her words. They stood in silence for several minutes before Ms. Gue knocked on the interrogation room door to let them know her client had been counseled.

Back in the room, Apollo kept his tone neutral but curious: "Lucy was a bit eccentric from what I've heard. What did you learn from keeping an eye on her?"

Burney looked at Ms. Gue who nodded for him to answer. He'd already admitted to following Lucy, so whatever he was going to say was likely going to be a mix of truth and damage control.

"Once a week she'd go to a mostly human-centric area of town in her human form. Sometimes she changed her clothes first, sometimes she didn't. I didn't see her talk with anyone. She sent a few messages on her phone but otherwise seemed to people watch. Edward guessed she enjoyed the anonymity of the experience." Burney shrugged as if it were an odd desire.

"But you kept following her?" Poppy asked from where she had resumed her earlier position leaning against the wall. Her voice held an aloofness that could be interpreted to imply that *all* the Montagues were beneath her notice if someone wanted to hear it that way. Her natural tone must have appealed to the Capulets.

"On occasion, as per Edward's request. He worried about his sister."

"Did anything catch your attention about Lucy's visit to Felix's Corner the day she died?" Apollo asked.

"*Walsh Capulet*," he said the name like it tasted bad, "walked in twenty or thirty minutes after Lucy had. *Also* in his human form. I didn't like that at all." Burney shook his head in disgust before frowning. "If I had done something, maybe I could have saved her."

"Tell us what happened," Apollo coaxed, ignoring the insinuation that Walsh had killed Lucy. What mattered was that the second door opening and closing in the recording was twenty-three minutes after Lucy's arrival, which lined up with Burney's twenty to thirty minutes estimate. That meant their murderer, not Walsh, came in silently after that or was hiding inside before Lucy arrived.

"Just the facts," Ms. Gue counseled Burney to ensure he didn't incriminate himself any further with his opinions about the Capulets as a whole.

Burney glanced at Poppy before choosing to pretend she didn't exist. "Well, I watched the tea cottage, expecting Lucy or that cat to hurry out. When they didn't, it occurred to me they could be in separate areas and not know the other was there. That, or they were both trying to be tolerant of one another by ignoring each other. Lucy was the type of person to think that was 'the high road.' Once I realized that, I went a few stores down to sit on a bench.

"But after a half hour, I heard a scream from the tea cottage," Burney continued. "I went up to the front porch to go inside, but through the door, I heard a woman hysterically yelling into the phone about having two dead people upstairs. Her description of the bodies told me it was Lucy and that cat. I immediately called Edward to let him know. Then, I went down the street and left."

"Why didn't you come forward earlier or tell us any of this yesterday?" Apollo asked. He was still scribbling down notes. He wanted to be angry with the dog hybrid, but he knew Burney would clam up if he showed even an ounce of judgement. They were lucky Ms. Gue wasn't muzzling Burney altogether.

"Edward thought it best to have me leave. I assumed he wasn't planning on telling you I was following Lucy. I wouldn't want to act against his wishes."

"And you didn't see anyone else go inside?" Poppy asked.

Ms. Gue nodded for Burney to answer, but Burney didn't bother looking at her.

"Once I realized they were in there ignoring each other and Lucy wasn't going to leave early, I didn't pay close attention. Lucy always stayed at these human places for over two hours, so why stare at the door?" Burney shrugged, clearly not upset about Lucy's death. Apollo guessed Burney discounted her as not a true Montague since she wasn't a purebred dog hybrid.

"Thanks for your help, Burney," Apollo said and stood up. He nodded at Ms. Gue. "Please stay here until we come back, or an officer shows you out. I want to double check a few things before you leave to make sure we don't need you to come in again."

Burney nodded and focused his attention on his pet dog in a way that made Apollo uncomfortable. Ms. Gue inclined her head and then frowned at Burney and his dog. Her brow was deeply furrowed, probably thinking through the possible things he and Poppy would be double checking.

Poppy led the way out, and they left the creepy hybrid and his lawyer behind. In the hallway, she tapped the folder of photos Apollo was still carrying and said, "I'm so glad I don't work with Montague Legacy Sports. Some of that family...." She shuddered. "Still, we should see if he has any recent photos of Lucy from his 'surveillance' and get a list of the places she went." She used air quotes around the word *surveillance*, completely encompassing Apollo's feelings about the situation.

Chapter 10

Poppy

The next morning at her desk, Poppy and Apollo poured over one of Lucy's photo albums. She had several of them full of her adventures, and they all had several pages for each trip. Her most recent album, however, only had a single photo per trip. Written below each photo was a date. Furthermore, there weren't any other photos from that date or a few days around that date on her computer or on her phone. Each photo in the album was of a desolate landscape or a sightseeing destination. Not one picture had a person in it.

After two hours of quietly arguing over each photo, Poppy and Apollo pieced together a partial list of places Lucy had gone, but only half of them had an obvious city she would have stayed in. Many of the places were easily accessible from a number of cities, which meant they didn't know where she might have stayed.

One photo in the album set off alarm bells.

"This one," Poppy said, tapping the third to last photo in the album — a breathtaking photo of tall plateaus jutting out of a wall of forest trees. The plateaus looked like jagged claws reaching out from a green-furred paw. Dramatic wispy clouds filled the sky above the plateaus and forest, making the photo worthy of an art gallery.

"That one?" Apollo sounded annoyed, but anyone could overhear them at her desk. He'd been making a point to sound aggravated, and despite knowing it was for show, Poppy was down to her last nerve. She didn't think she could keep up the ruse much longer. She didn't even want to. Not only was her mind replaying their almost kiss in his car, but she was worrying about what this case was doing to Apollo professionally. She wanted Apollo to stop acting and be himself.

"Last night, I did some research on West Pukanto," Poppy explained as patiently as she could while their dynamic weighed down on her. "Where Mallary suspects the knife is from. These are the Pukanto Plateaus. The only trailhead that leads to them is in West Pukanto. Lucy has definitely been there. Apparently, as recently as two months ago."

While Apollo added the location to their list, Poppy pulled up West Pukanto on her computer. It was fourteen hours away from Spoville by car or a three-hour flight.

"That's not overly helpful," Apollo said as he looked at the map. Poppy had to agree. There were three towns and two larger cities nearby that people often stayed in. To make matters worse, they'd found camping gear in Lucy's garage. Who knew if she even stayed in the towns or cities?

"Well, it's something," Poppy said in her most measured voice.

Apollo grunted noncommittally in response.

They didn't have any luck pinpointing the locations of the last two photos in the album. Still, they had uncovered over a dozen locations Lucy had visited. There were just as many photos that they hadn't had any luck figuring out, but Poppy was confident that circulating them around the police department would get most of them identified after a day or three. However, she hoped she didn't need to keep working with Apollo for another three days.

After they finished the album, Apollo excused himself and went to Montague Legacy Sports to get a recent photo of Lucy from Burney's surveillance. Poppy was more than happy to let Apollo go back to that hellhole alone. She just wished she had an excuse to make herself scarce as well. She didn't want to talk to anyone. Especially to anyone who had been watching her and Apollo the last few days.

Poppy pulled up the pre-Crisis photo of Walsh and tried to make herself look busy by adding a few gray and white streaks to Walsh's hair to update the photo and make him look a little more like he did when he died — minus the slit throat.

Apparently, she didn't seem busy enough. Like the evening before, when Apollo left earlier than her, her desk was swarmed the instant he left the building. Everyone wanted to give her their two cents about her *temporary* partner. Poppy did her best to remain as professional as possible and deflect the conversations, but it didn't matter. If she got one person to leave, someone else took their place.

She didn't know if she should be relieved or not when Apollo returned. She didn't want more fodder for gossip, but he was her escape plan; he'd messaged her to be ready to go out and check on the leads he'd gotten from Burney. Poppy never thought she'd be thankful for Burney, but today she was.

They only stayed in the building long enough to leave a copy of the latest photo of Lucy with Officers Kent and Cane, who were still assisting them with the case. The two officers would get the photo to the police departments on their list — West Pukanto first — to see if anyone remembered Lucy visiting in her human or hybrid form. They were also sending Walsh's photos just in case a connection could be found there. It seemed like a long shot that someone would remember a passing tourist, but it was something. Hopefully knowing the dates Lucy had been to each location would help jog someone's memory.

Lucy favored cash and never charged anything to a card that could leave a financial trail for them to follow. Sending out the photos was their best bet. While Officers Kent and Cane spent the afternoon on that, Poppy and Apollo would canvas the different areas Burney said he'd followed Lucy to.

Poppy forced herself to walk at a normal speed out of the building. She felt like every eye was on her and Apollo. The eyes stayed on just her when Captain Starl called Apollo into his office for a quick word. She didn't wait for Apollo, but instead continued out of the building and away from her concerned colleagues.

Outside, she took deep breaths and looked at the trees lining the parking lot. Thankfully, none of her colleagues followed her out. She had five entire minutes to herself before Apollo hurried out and unlocked the car. They had both known he couldn't give her his car keys when he got stopped; that would have fallen into the trusting and friendly category. As it was, Poppy couldn't get into his cedar-scented car fast enough.

Poppy tipped the passenger seat back as he started driving. Her head throbbed from being in the station all morning. She'd never had a problem spending a half or full day doing desk work for a case. That was, of course, before everyone had seen her and Apollo bickering. The first day or two, she had needed to remind herself that Apollo was egging her on for show; it had been the only thing that stopped her from being pulled before a judge and trying to plead that her owl-instincts overwhelmed her. It would have been a bullshit plea; no one's hybrid instincts overwhelmed them. But her issue today wasn't related to holding back from tearing Apollo into bite-size pieces. Not. At. All.

The problem was everyone else.

"So," Apollo said. His voice was full of energy. "Ms. Gue had Burney write down all the places he followed Lucy to when she shifted to her human form. None of the places are near the Montague Stadium or offices. Interestingly, none of them are downtown either."

"Downtown doesn't fit Lucy's eclectic tastes from what I saw in the pictures of her condo," Poppy said, not bothering to open her eyes. She wished they'd been able to go to Lucy's in person instead of being sent home after the explosion. She'd liked the look of it. It seemed peaceful. Poppy could use some peaceful right about now.

"Are you okay?"

Poppy opened her eyes to glance over at Apollo, who was shooting her a worried look that reminded her of what he was like around his brother — nice, not a dick, and passionate about people respecting her.

"Are *you*?" she asked back. "Are you going to be able to recover from this case?"

The sheer number of officers, detectives, and techs that had come and spoken to her about Apollo's "abhorrent attitude" and her own "upright professionalism" — Mallary's words just that morning — was driving her up the wall. When Apollo had avoided her, no one had said anything. Most people hadn't even noticed. Now, everyone was talking about the two of them, and everyone was siding with her. While it was true that Apollo was instigating and playing his part well, it annoyed Poppy that he was burning bridges and possibly irreparably damaging his reputation as a respectable detective.

"What do you mean?" His nose wrinkled, twitching his whiskers around, and his ears drooped a little.

Poppy shifted to her human form, hoping Apollo would follow suit; she hadn't quite learned to read his face in his hybrid mouse form. Luckily, he shifted too. Now, Poppy could see that Apollo truly had no idea what she was talking about.

"I've had three separate people come up and admit to me that if they were me, you'd be maimed by now. They wanted to know how I have been able to, and I quote, 'not garrote him with his own tail,' and they hadn't thought 'anything could be narrower, but apparently his views of others are, in fact, narrower than his tail.' Over half of the department has come and spoken to me about how horrible you are."

Apollo slowed down for a red light, unseeing. Poppy was pretty sure he was driving on autopilot at this point. "What?"

"Even people who've worked with you have commented to me about your sudden change of spirit. You've never had a problem working with women. You've interviewed bird hybrids without shooting barbs at them. You've, apparently, dated a cat hybrid or two with only complimentary things to say about them once they had become your exes. They're saying this change in your attitude is worrisome, and they aren't sure they want to work with you again."

Apollo gawked at her. "Before we left, the captain literally congratulated me at keeping up such an argumentative front."

"Yeah, but Captain Starl knows what you're doing. Does he know I know what you're doing?"

"I don't know. When did everyone talk to you? We've been together constantly since the case started." The car drove forward when the light turned green, and Poppy considered suggesting they pull over.

"You left before me last night," she pointed out, scanning the street more carefully than she normally did as a passenger. "A number of them spoke to me then. A few people have stopped me when I've gotten up from my desk throughout the morning, and more people came over to me when you left the building to get the photo of Lucy."

"I did see you stopping to talk to a lot of people when you got up," Apollo muttered as he pulled into the parking area of a small shopping center with several stores and restaurants that didn't cater to hybrid tastes.

Poppy assumed that this was an area Burney had mentioned; she hadn't seen the list yet. When she'd moved to the area, she had looked in at the shops here because they had such idyllic and fanciful window displays. The ones that sold clothing, however, didn't have any tops that would let her shift into her hybrid form without suffocating the feathers on her arms. The pants situation in the stores wasn't much better even if she didn't have a feathered tail like some bird hybrids did. None of the restaurants had any dishes with insects or additives that were reptile, amphibian, or rodent flavored. The dishes they served might be just fine, but they'd never hit the spot for her.

"I had assumed," Poppy said after they sat in silence for over a minute, "that Captain Starl had been talking to you about the problem when he asked for a word in his office."

"And this, everyone's opinion about me," Apollo's voice wavered as he turned to look at Poppy, "is why you're upset?"

"Yeah," Poppy's eyebrows shot up. She'd thought that was obvious. They couldn't let this ruin his career. They needed to do something. And soon.

Apollo nodded slowly while looking at her intently for longer than seemed normal. He turned to face forward again, still nodding.

"We need a plan," Poppy said, reaching out and touching his hand on the stick shift again, even though she was trying to physically keep her distance. "You can't let being the Montagues' preferred detective stain your career."

"My current plan is to not go back to the station today. I'll mull over the issue tonight. For now, let's go flash photos around and see if anyone remembers seeing Lucy."

Poppy let their focus switch to the work at hand, though she thought they should prioritize making a plan of attack regarding his career sooner than later. It was unlikely Captain Starl would fire Apollo for following orders, but if someone reported Apollo to internal affairs for unprofessionalism — and there were a *lot* of moments to choose from — this case would, at the very least, be a black mark on Apollo's record. She liked him too much to let him permanently sweep the issue under the rug, but they still had work to do.

When they walked into the first restaurant, Baudelaire, Apollo smiled at the hostess and flashed his badge. Poppy could tell he forced the smile, but she didn't say anything. Instead, she pulled the photos of Lucy and Walsh out and showed them to the hostess and a few of the waitstaff. No one recognized Lucy, but one of them said a man who looked like Walsh might have come in one night a few months back. He wasn't sure and couldn't remember who the man had been dining with. The staff at the next five places in the area didn't recognize Lucy or Walsh. Their seventh and final stop had someone who remembered Lucy — she had eaten her lunch alone on both her visits and hadn't spoken to anyone — but they didn't recognize Walsh.

Poppy suggested that she drive them to the next human centric area on the list. Apollo shrugged and tossed her the keys, which was a blaring sign that he was bothered by what she had told him. He clearly didn't want to talk about it yet, so she drove in silence and let him brood next to her. She hadn't come up with any ideas yet to remedy what had become a glaring Capulet-Montague problem for Apollo.

Thirty minutes later, Poppy pulled into a parking structure and scanned for an open space. On the third level, she pulled into an empty spot, between a blue sedan and a massive purple SUV. Apollo still hadn't spoken.

"Do you know which part of the mall we're going to?" Poppy asked. She remembered that the shops that didn't cater to hybrids were grouped near one of the larger department stores, but which one eluded her.

Apollo took a deep breath before saying, "Oddly, the human-centric shops are all next to Hybrid Hookup."

Hybrid Hookup was the first new department store to open up after the Crisis. It had clothing basics that would fit almost any hybrid. They even divided the store into sections that accounted for shifted tail thickness and the amount of wing you had — slightly larger than normal arms like Poppy's to wings that stretched all the way down a hybrid's side and were capable of sustaining flight. Poppy particularly appreciated the shoe department since her feet went from a normal size eight to a talon size eight, which accounted for her new foot shape. The store had locations all over, but some smaller towns were campaigning against it in order to bring back boutiques and mom-and-pop shops.

"If you share your thoughts, I might be able to help," Poppy said as they walked through the mall towards the far end where Hybrid Hookup was.

"The previous Capulet-preferred detective, Nigel Brothers, had a reputation for being ornery and rude, but to everyone. He got the job done, but no one liked him."

"Do you think Captain Starl told him what he told you?"

"Or the captain's predecessor did," Apollo agreed as they walked by a Birman Folds storefront and Scot's Byss storefront side by side in the mall. Poppy hadn't thought the two Capulet stores were ever in the same location, much less *that* close to one another. "If Detective Brothers chose to be rude and difficult all the time rather than just when a Capulet/Montague-adjacent case came up," Apollo continued, "then he would have protected his reputation as impartial and getting the job done."

"True. But being unpleasant all the time sounds exhausting." Poppy grimaced at the idea.

"Unless he was like that naturally," Apollo said. "That's the first human-centric shop." He pointed to a clothing boutique past Maud's Plants, which was a store that specialized in helping hybrids find the right plants for their houses that wouldn't irritate their senses.

It wasn't until their third stop in the mall that something came of their search.

"Oh yeah, I recognize them," the waiter at Flaky Pastry said.

"You do? Both of them?" Poppy asked to be certain.

"Yeah. The woman came in a handful of times, but the man just twice, I think. Both times, they sat in the booth in the back corner." The back corner booth was the least desirable location as it was right where the bathroom door opened, but it also wasn't visible from outside Flaky Pastry.

"Together?" Apollo asked.

"Yeah." The waiter nodded firmly. "Though," he paused for a second, "they didn't enter or leave together. The woman was here for a good thirty or more minutes before he joined her. I remember because she seemed calmer on the two days he stopped by."

Poppy and Apollo exchanged a look. Other than dying together, this was the first time anyone had made a firm connection between Lucy and Walsh. Like Felix's Corner, this location didn't have a single item in its display or on its menu that would tempt a hybrid. Unlike the tea cottage, it was an upscale location. The wooden furniture might have been teak, and the booths were upholstered in a soft burgundy. Poppy thought the accents around the pastry display might have actually been gilded.

"Did you hear anything they talked about? Notice anything else about them?" she asked.

"Not particularly," the waiter said. "I got the feeling that they didn't want to be bothered. I mostly left them alone and checked in minimally."

After thanking the waiter for his help, Poppy and Apollo checked the rest of the stores that didn't cater to hybrids and found one more that reported almost the same thing as Flaky Pastry. Lucy had been there several times alone, and Walsh had joined her once. The waitress at the second place had noticed Walsh because he dressed like a walking mannequin from Scot's Byss, where her boyfriend liked to shop.

"They knew each other," Apollo said as he sat down in the driver's seat of his car.

"They knew each other well," Poppy amended.

"But no one in their families mentioned that."

"The times they were remembered just in this one area spanned an entire year," Poppy continued.

"If what we're piecing together about Lucy is right, she was trying to hide this from her family. She was secretly shifting to her human form and visiting areas that hybrids don't frequent all that often."

"Her distant cousin Burney was following her, but not all the time. He only saw her meet with Walsh on the day they died," Apollo continued her trail of thought.

"But Lucy seemed to go to a lot of these places alone several times *before* Walsh would join her."

"He probably joined her on days she knew she wasn't being followed," Apollo finished.

They both sat in Apollo's car silently for a bit while that sunk in. Lucy and Walsh knew someone was following Lucy, possibly even who. Then, they ended up dead together. While Burney would make a great suspect, he could be seen on a traffic cam video on a bench like he said he was, typing away on his phone until he ran toward Tanya's scream. He didn't do it. There had to be someone else who knew Lucy and Walsh were getting together and didn't like it. Maybe someone else was following them, too.

There were still a lot of pieces of the puzzle missing.

Chapter 11

Apollo

Apollo forced himself to look at his desk and at his computer. Nowhere else. Now that he knew people were watching him and Poppy, and not with an indulgent frame of mind, he could feel the pervasive disapproval in the air. He had never felt so self-conscious before. He didn't know what to do or what to think.

Not only had Poppy let him in on the fact that he was losing everyone's trust, but her priority was making sure *he* was okay. After they'd finished visiting the different places on Burney's list, they'd gone back to his place and spent the last hour of the workday without everyone watching his every action as they tried to piece together what they knew. Then, Poppy had stayed for another two hours and insisted they find a way to save his reputation. She refused to accept that he'd take care of it on his own. They, however, hadn't come up with any solutions.

And now? Now, he didn't know if her resting her hand on his shoulder as she leaned over him to look at the two schedules he had spread out was a ploy to help his image or something more. Like maybe a desire to touch him or be close to him.

He knew that had to be wishful thinking. Poppy had been nothing but professional around him, even when concerned about his career. To top off his confusion, she'd completely ignored the fact that he and Orion had talked about her and that he'd described her as pretty. And might have completely missed that he'd been thinking about kissing her when he had brought her back to the station. She hadn't hinted at either once. She'd been perfectly professional. He had no indication that she might be interested in more. He was just projecting his own desires onto her actions.

"You're seeing what I'm seeing, right?" Poppy's breath tickled his ear.

Apollo cleared his throat and blinked several times at the schedules. "Maybe," he said as he focused back on the way they'd color coded Lucy and Walsh's calendars.

"Every vacation or extended weekend Walsh took in the last year lines up with times Lucy was on one of her road trips." Poppy reached past him and started pointing out the days that lined up. She put a little more weight on her hand, and Apollo could swear he felt her body heat through the back of his shirt. Her pine needle perfume had him by the throat.

"But Lucy also has a lot more small road trips marked on her schedule," Apollo managed to say.

"True, but it seems like she might have had more flexibility in her schedule than Walsh. His job as a CEO might not have allowed him to travel as much. If she drove and he met her there for the weekend or something…" Poppy's voice trailed off.

Apollo nodded, but stopped when his car brushed the feathers on Poppy's cheek.

"I'll pull up Walsh's finances," Apollo said. "We already know Lucy used cash and had her phone off on her trips. There's no way to track her movements. Maybe Walsh wasn't as circumspect."

"You start on that while I give Jennifer Capulet a call and see if she can shed any light on her uncle's travels. She'd been around him more than the rest of the family recently." She stood up, depriving him of her hand on his shoulder. "I'll request the cell phone data for Walsh's phone; we can see if his GPS tracking follows a similar pattern of blackouts or left a trail, assuming he took it with him."

Poppy walked off toward her desk, and Apollo forced himself not to watch her. Who knew what everyone would think if he admired the peculiar way she half hopped every few steps and glided a little until her foot landed next. Would they think he was leering at her and add that to the list of his egregious behavior that week?

He sighed and started digging into Walsh's finances, both personal and business. They were lucky that they already had access since the Capulets wanted answers even faster than the Montagues did; the bomb that went off in Walsh's townhouse had added the impetus the family needed to cooperate fully with the investigation despite "the Montagues' detective" working on the case.

Apollo skimmed through the documents searching for any out-of-town expenditures. Rather than keeping an ear open to the station chatter, Apollo let the task at hand take all his attention. He didn't want to hear what people were saying today.

For a while, there were only a few out-of-town charges here and there and mostly on Walsh's business account. Then, about fifteen months ago, a few more started popping up on his personal account, too. Apollo made a list of places, especially hotel and rental charges, with the dates.

At about the year mark, Walsh's trips stopped including car rentals, even the slightly longer stays. The places didn't exactly match the list of the places from Lucy's photo album, but Apollo thought a few of the names were familiar; they might be from surrounding towns and cities he and Poppy had seen in their search but thought were too far from the photo locations. Many people traveled out to see things. And in Lucy and Walsh's case, if they were together, they'd want to stay in areas where they'd draw the least attention.

"Jennifer Capulet is going to come in and talk with us. She was on her way to a meeting nearby and will stop by when that finishes since she didn't have time to talk." Poppy said as she sat down in a chair next to Apollo's desk. He'd been so engrossed in his task he hadn't seen or heard her coming. A glance at the clock on the wall told him she'd been gone for over forty-five minutes. He was noticeably disappointed that she hadn't chosen to lean over him again and fill the air with her pine needle scent.

Apollo frowned at the thought, but the significance of Poppy's absence took on a new meaning the more he thought about it. Normally, in a forty-five-minute time frame, someone might have spoken to him. He was working hard; it was plausible that no one would interrupt him. He shouldn't take that to heart. However, not one person at work, other than Poppy, had spoken to him beyond responding if he spoke to them first. Apollo had never kept track, but he thought that normally a half-dozen people would have spoken to him in the few hours he'd been there. He was social, but other people often came to him first. No one had today.

"She said she'd be happy to stay out of the office a little longer and avoid her new CEO duties for a bit," Poppy continued. "She sounded exhausted."

"Can't be easy taking over suddenly," Apollo muttered. He'd panic about the sudden death of his reputation later. Pushing his first page of notes over to Poppy, he asked, "Do you recognize any of these places?"

"No," she said after a minute or two. "Do these specific dates line up with Lucy's travels?"

"I haven't checked yet, but here," he leaned over and circled the dates for a week stay in Rafity City, "he stopped doing car rentals on most of his trips."

"That city has good public transport," Poppy murmured, "but I'm guessing a lot of these are smaller towns and wouldn't have as great of a system. What do the two colors mean?"

"I wrote trips paid on the business accounts in black and the personal ones in blue."

They split the list and worked on seeing what attractions might be near each of Walsh's trips. A half-dozen matched up easily with Lucy's identified photos. Three others were close to other photos but would have required a long drive to visit. What they were finding added up to one thing.

Apollo glanced at Poppy to see her nodding her head as she noted down another commonality. A movement behind her caught his eye, and he saw Officer Cane wave at them and point toward the conference room.

"Could Jennifer be here?" Apollo asked Poppy. "Officer Cane is pointing at the conference room."

Poppy blinked at her watch in surprise. "I thought she'd be another thirty minutes, but it could be her. I'll go see. If it's her, I'll wave you over." She stood up and left.

Apollo rubbed his eyebrows and glanced around. A few people looked away when his eyes crossed theirs, but a handful of others shook their heads at him in open disappointment. He felt like he couldn't breathe. He hadn't come up with any solutions for fixing his reputation after Poppy left his house the night before, regardless of how late he had stayed up mulling over the issue.

All morning, he'd toned back the arguing and baiting of Poppy, but the two of them had mostly been working quietly together. It was unlikely that anyone knew he wasn't being rude to her or difficult to work with. Even if he didn't do anything more to follow the captain's orders, the damage was done. Without directly addressing the issue, which would defeat his orders in the first place and all the effort he'd put in over the years to avoid Poppy and get the Montagues to trust him, everyone would remember these past few days of him acting out of character. None of his colleagues would trust him completely again on the off chance he gave a repeat performance.

Feeling defeated, Apollo looked over at the conference room. Poppy lifted her chin when he caught her eye. Jennifer Capulet had indeed arrived.

Apollo got up and headed straight for Poppy. He pretended to be unaffected by everyone's opinions of him and said a few cheerful hellos. Before joining Poppy in the conference room, he straightened his shoulders and pushed all of his work drama away.

At the sight of the empty conference table, Apollo looked to the far end of the room. Poppy was standing next to Jennifer by the coffee bar. They were both fixing cups of coffee and looking worlds apart. Poppy was in black slacks and a blue sweater — very business casual and normal detective clothing, if still more attractive than what other detectives wore. Jennifer, on the other hand, was in a perfectly tailored, hot pink business dress. Her hair was half up in a hairdo that Apollo had seen at weddings and such but didn't know the name of. Her dark ears barely peeked out from the curls on top of her head. Apollo couldn't see Jennifer's feet, but he knew she had heels on since she was taller than Poppy today. The Capulet family lawyer was nowhere in sight, but then again, Jennifer was trying to escape the trappings of her new job, so coming alone had probably greatly appealed to her.

"How do you take your coffee, Detective Pinon?" Poppy asked when the door clicked closed behind him.

"With moth cream and white cheddar whip on top, please," he answered since she was already holding a cup for him.

Drinks in hand, they all sat down at the far end of the conference table near the coffee bar. Apollo suppressed the hum of pleasure he had at his first sip. Most people didn't put in enough moth cream and put too much cheese whip on top, but Poppy had gotten it just right. He fought the urge to lean to his right and be a little closer to her.

"How's the first week been going?" Poppy asked.

"We've managed to move the upcoming business trips to my fourth and fifth weeks of work instead of next week. That's something," Jennifer sighed more than said. "Otherwise, besides taking care of actual business tasks, I'm drowning in paperwork for the new position." She sat slumped in her chair, creating wrinkles throughout her dress.

"That sounds rough," Poppy commiserated. "How did your Uncle Walsh balance all the work and having time for himself?"

Apollo had to admit that Poppy did a great job pointing Jennifer to what they wanted to know. He was more than happy to follow her lead.

"He didn't," Jennifer said. "At least, he didn't before I started taking over some of his tasks. When I was interning, he would take one weekend for himself a month. That was it, and he generally spent it at home, I think. He worked more or less every other day of the month, like my dad."

"Your dad is the CEO of your family's other brand of stores, Birman Folds, right?" Apollo asked, even though he knew the information.

Jennifer and Poppy both nodded to confirm.

"And are you starting as CEO at Scot's Byss before eventually taking over from your dad at Birman Folds? That's the larger brand of the two I thought."

"Thankfully, my older brother will be CEO of that one. Even without taking over yet, Tristan is already working fifty-hour weeks."

Apollo nodded as if he'd known she had an older brother, which he hadn't. He didn't remember interviewing a Tristan Capulet, but that didn't mean they hadn't. They'd interviewed over a dozen Capulets the day after the explosion. It could be that her brother just hadn't stood out.

"When you started helping Walsh, you noticed he took more time for himself?" Poppy redirected the conversation to the topic they needed to know about.

"Yeah. He did a good job of not overloading me, but much sooner than any of us thought, he started putting me in charge for a week every other month and disappearing, extending his weekend off by a day or two or adding weekends to his business trips and staying in those places."

"Was everyone okay with this change?" Poppy asked.

"My dad was perplexed by it, but he acknowledged it was good training for my future as CEO. At first, my mom didn't care one way or another, but then again, she doesn't do much with the business and focuses more on the cat shows and breeding. Though, after six-ish months, she got irritable every time one of Uncle Walsh's trips was mentioned." Jennifer shifted in her seat and tipped her head back. At first, Apollo thought she was staring at the ceiling, but after she released a large sigh, he saw her eyes were closed. She was so run down she was taking this as an opportunity to rest.

She continued talking without opening her eyes: "Originally, I thought she was envious and wanted my dad to do the same, but then, I heard her say that Uncle Walsh was making idiotic choices and was ruining everything. I don't know exactly what that was about. My dad and Uncle Walsh had hammered out all the details to their satisfaction after three months of his trips."

Apollo forced himself not to exchange a glance with Poppy. It sounded to him like Jennifer's mother, Nancy Capulet, hadn't told them everything during her interview the day after Walsh's town-house exploded. She'd seemed distraught, but any nervousness she'd shown had been attributed to Jennifer being near the explosion. They'd missed that she knew something. They'd missed that Nancy thought her brother-in-law was making a stupid mistake. She knew more about the trips than just the fact that they were happening. She might have known that her brother-in-law was consorting with a Montague. Poppy had to see that too.

"Your uncle was the only one of his generation who wasn't married, right?" Poppy asked. Apollo tried to remember who would be in that grouping. There were Jennifer's parents, Charles and Nancy. Walsh was Charles's only brother, but Apollo thought he heard something about a cousin that was the original financial backer for the stores but didn't live locally — a Scottish Fold hybrid whose name Apollo couldn't remember.

Jennifer nodded.

"Do you know if he dated or was ever serious with anyone?"

Apollo watched Jennifer out of the corner of his eye while he pretended to focus on his coffee more than her. At Poppy's question, Jennifer eyes flew open, and her ears disappeared completely into her curls as they twisted back against her head. Her breathing rate increased, and she looked more than a little panicked. Apollo imagined she had gone pale beneath her fur.

"You— you want to know if he was dating Lucy Montague?" she asked. Her voice rose to a squeak on the name "Montague." Apollo thought it noteworthy that she'd jumped directly to that conclusion.

"Do you know of any connection between the two of them?" Poppy pushed. "Did you ever see them together?"

"I—" Jennifer swallowed hard, and her tone turned a little dead. "I've never heard anything about my uncle's personal life. I don't know if he dated, but I've seen his calendar; he didn't have the time, b—" She cut herself off. It was obvious she'd just connected the dots; her uncle had the time once she'd started taking work off his plate. She glanced between Poppy and Apollo, and her tone turned defeated: "You two know our families. Dating between our families…"

"Wouldn't be tolerated?" Apollo supplied.

She gave him the smallest nod.

"If your Uncle Walsh and Lucy were seeing each other, romantically or not, would someone in your family do something about it?"

Jennifer squeezed her lips together in a thin line. Her voice was reed thin as she forced herself to answer. "I don't know. Certain family members on each side seem to particularly hate the others." Her eyes were squeezed shut at this point and her breathing shallow. Apollo wondered if she was regretting not bringing the family lawyer to make this more official and save her from these questions or relieved to not be scrutinized here as well as at work.

"We're going to ask that you don't share what we talked about with your family," Poppy told Jennifer. "If we find that there is any credence to these ideas, we'll be the ones to say something. You don't need to bring this up with them and deal with fielding their thoughts on this. That's what *we're* here for."

Still looking panicked, Jennifer gave a jerky nod before she practically ran out of the police station. Apollo hoped she'd call in sick and take the rest of the day off. He doubted she could hide how freaked out she was.

In the partial privacy of the conference room, Apollo and Poppy finished their coffees. They didn't talk for the moment, and Apollo spent the time trying to brace himself to go back out under the watchful eyes of their colleagues. He'd rather go somewhere and be with Poppy, but he knew that wasn't in the cards.

Poppy's phone dinged. A second later, Apollo's did too. They both read their messages. Mallary had found fingerprints on the propane tank and one of the bomb components from Walsh's townhouse. They stood and threw out their empty coffee cups, and Apollo wondered which family member the new evidence would point them at.

Chapter 12

Jennifer

It had been three days since Detectives Barrdom and Pinon had more than hinted that Uncle Walsh and Miles's Aunt Lucy had been dating, and Jennifer couldn't take it anymore. Her mom had come by the office yesterday and sauntered around looking at this and that, and all Jennifer could think about was how much her mom openly loathed the Montagues. Then, this morning, her dad had come by to see if she had any questions. Her brother had popped into her office after lunch to show her how to do something she'd admitted to her dad she didn't know how to do. Logically, she knew her family was trying to support her through this difficult transition, but that wasn't what her brain was telling her.

Her brain said that she was being watched. That they knew what she was doing behind their back. She needed to get away. Get away before someone noticed what she was up to.

Slipping her phone off her desk, she held it in her lap and discreetly sent a text like she was breaking the rules in school.

Caffeine Rush 330.

Easing her phone back onto her desk, Jennifer looked at her computer screen and tried to make sense of the budget in front of her. Uncle Walsh had taught her the ins and outs of Scot's Byss's books, but today, instead of seeing the numbers, she saw the reflection of the clouds in the sky outside. The floor-to-ceiling windows of her office — the entire left wall — mocked her, telling her she would be held back from everything she could see by a thin veil. Her right was also a wall of windows, but into the office. From where she sat, she could see three cousins and an aunt, which meant that they could see her too. She needed to keep it together.

Ten minutes later, she feigned a migraine. She told her assistant that she was calling it quits for the day and heading out. Her assistant shot her a sympathetic smile and didn't ask her any further questions. She probably knew where Jennifer was going.

Jennifer shook her head at the thought. She was being paranoid, but she couldn't shake the feeling after talking with the detectives. Her assistant couldn't really know where she was going. As Jennifer left the office, she was certain everyone watched her. Which they probably did; she was a young, untried CEO thrust to the top through nepotism. But what if that wasn't why they were looking at her?

Once outside of the Scot's Byss offices, Jennifer walked three blocks towards her apartment before turning left and heading another four blocks to the park. She thought she was walking at her normal pace, but she couldn't be sure. She crossed the park, pretending to admire the blooming flowers as she scanned for anyone she recognized. Not seeing any familiar faces, she took the path that wound through the trees. When no one could see her, she shifted to her human form. Not even her closest friends would recognize her face now. She was still dressed like herself, but there was nothing she could do about that. On the far side of the park, she grabbed a taxi to Caffeine Rush.

Twenty-five minutes later, she handed the driver cash for her ride and climbed out. She knew she shouldn't be here, but she also knew that she'd come again without a second thought.

Three of the ten outside tables had groups of people drinking and chatting at them; the other seven were empty. The front windows of the coffee shop were too reflective to see much of the interior, so she headed toward the door to check if Miles had already arrived and was inside; this coffee shop was closer to his office than hers. Before she reached it, the door opened, and he stepped out holding two drinks.

Miles smiled at her and then immediately frowned. He set the to-go drinks down on an empty table next to the door and took off the black sweatshirt he was wearing. The long sleeve shirt he had on underneath it was blue rather than red; he'd taken the time to do more than throw on a hoodie to cover one of the Montague red shirts he wore to work.

Holding the sweatshirt out to her, he said, "Put this on."

Without questioning him, Jennifer took it and slipped it on over her purple silk blouse and pink cardigan. He'd given her his coat the last two times they'd met, and she hadn't cared that it looked ridiculous over her flowing skirt or hot pink dress. She was adjusting the sleeves so that they weren't twisted on her arms when she felt Miles slide his fingers through her hair, ruining the carefully grouped curls that had survived most of the day.

"Thanks," she said. She almost didn't want to keep a change of clothes handy for when they met up, even if it would be safer. Then, he might not give her his jacket each time. She imagined Miles wore the honey-scented cologne she smelled on his jackets just to put her at ease. If that was the case, it was working; she felt safe wrapped in his jacket and by his side.

"No problem." Miles reached for the drinks and handed her one. "Frothy steamed milk," he said. "Now, tell me what's wrong. If stepping into your uncle's shoes is taking this much of a toll on you, you need to tell your dad no. You shouldn't have had to put in ten-hour days this past weekend. It's Monday, and you're already run down."

"Like you're telling your dad no," she scoffed. "But it's not work that has me freaking out."

"It's us meeting up?" Miles asked. He wrapped his arm around her and led her to the table inside where they'd sat the last time they'd gotten together. It was away from the front door and windows.

"Yes, but it's more than that." Jennifer slid onto the bench and pulled Miles in next to her instead of letting him sit across the table like he'd done before. She didn't want to talk too loudly. "The detectives asked me more questions Friday afternoon." She'd kept that to herself. She hadn't told him she was going straight to the police station after meeting with him.

Originally, she hadn't wanted the murders to intrude on them getting to know each other, but since then... she'd almost told Miles in their text chats over the weekend, but she was worried that someone would read her messages. She had no reason to think that, but she couldn't risk it. She didn't even have Miles in her phone as Miles. He was "Smile," which wasn't creative since it was just a shift of one letter, but at least his name wouldn't pop up on her screen for anyone to see. She needed to talk to someone about what she'd learned, and Miles was the only person who'd understand.

"Do you think they found out about us and are going to tell our parents? I don't think Detective Pinon would mention it. He's too level-headed and perceptive to do that." He was trying to comfort her, which was sweet, but that wasn't the issue.

"No, it was about Uncle Walsh and Lucy."

Miles watched her intently, patiently waiting for her to continue.

"Detectives Barrdom and Pinon think they were dating." He tensed beside her and pulled her a little closer. Jennifer spoke as fast as she could to get the admission over with: "At least, I think that's what they think. They didn't deny it when I asked if that was what they were asking me. They told me not to say anything to my family about their line of questioning."

"Aunt Lucy never mentioned dating anyone, but if it wasn't serious, I don't see why she'd say something to me. And if she was dating your uncle... then I can understand why she *would* keep it to herself."

"Let's assume they were dating," Jennifer whispered. She took a sip of her milk before blurting out, "Do you think anyone in your family would... you know... kill them? 'Cause I would like to think no one in my family would, but I can't, in all honesty, commit to that."

"I don't think so," Miles said after taking a long moment to think about it. "But I did tell the detectives that Aunt Lucy thought she was being followed before she died."

"Are *you* being followed?" Jennifer's hands shook so badly at the thought that she had to set down her drink; she didn't want to spill it on herself or Miles.

"No," Miles said with certainty and grabbed ahold of her shaking hands. He'd answered so firmly that she turned a little to look at him. He grimaced and added, "But I drove a circuitous route to get here on purpose and may have rigged my car to drop a fake license plate over my real one with the push of a button."

Shit. That sounded very illegal.

"You've seriously considered it then." Jennifer stared at her drink next to their entwined hands but didn't pick it back up again.

"Being followed, yes. Though I wasn't worried that someone might kill us for seeing each other," Miles muttered.

"It's highly distressing that we can't rule it out, huh?"

Miles pulled her back against him, and she rested her head on his shoulder as they both stared at their drinks. Their sad, non-hybrid bent drinks.

She took a deep breath, pulling more of the comforting honey scent into her nose. She didn't know what they could do. They had agreed immediately that the only shot they had was to try to see each other in their human forms. Over the last decade, they'd changed a lot since they were kids, and no one would recognize them from before the Crisis. But if either of them were followed or someone noticed them wearing the same clothes as before they shifted, then it'd be over. She was sure Miles had paid for their drinks with cash, like she'd paid for her taxi with cash.

Both their phones buzzed with messages at nearly the same time, and Jennifer lifted her head up. Neither of them reached for their phones. They just sat there.

"I read the last dire message first," Jennifer forced her tone to be light. "I guess it's your turn."

In unamused agreement, Miles reached out and picked his phone up from the table. "It's from my dad again." He looked at her, and she nodded for him to open it. His head tilted to the side as he read the message. "Detective Pinon has asked our family to meet him at town hall in the assembly room."

Jennifer grabbed her phone and read her message. "My dad says that Detective Barrdom wants to update our family on the investigation," she looked at Miles, "at town hall in the assembly room."

"In two hours?"

"In two hours," Jennifer echoed.

"Well, since we have two hours, let's go get something to eat."

"You aren't going back to work?"

Both previous rendezvous, they'd talked for thirty minutes or an hour and each gone back to work, or in Jennifer's case on Friday, the police station. However, those short meeting times were enough for her to decide that she liked him. At school, they'd been a year apart and never interacted for obvious reasons. Now, she knew they had a ton in common and were dealing with similar family issues and ridiculous work pressures. Miles understood her in a way other people their age couldn't.

She still couldn't get over the fact that he'd used her number after he realized she was, well, who she was. But then again, she'd known who he was from the moment he'd introduced himself, and she had given him her number anyway. They'd messaged each other every day since Uncle Walsh's townhouse had exploded, met up twice last week, and today was only Monday and they'd already met up again.

"No, I won't be able to focus. I'll say I'm taking a late lunch." He gave her that dopey grin he had that was so hard to say no to.

"You haven't had lunch?" Jennifer checked the time on her phone. It was 3:45 in the afternoon. When Miles shook his head, she asked, "Okay, where do you want to go?"

They grabbed their drinks, and Miles led her to his car. She raised her eyebrow at him when she saw his sporty convertible — luckily in black rather than in Montague red like his dad's. The car screamed family money which clashed with how down to earth Miles was. He shrugged and opened the door for her. Smiling and rolling her eyes, she climbed in.

Miles drove them fifteen minutes out of town to a burger joint she'd never heard of, but the food was great. He had the elk burger, and she'd had a tuna burger. Jennifer could tell Miles was trying to keep her distracted, which she appreciated. On her own, she'd be spiraling about what the detectives were going to tell them all.

The detectives had to be revealing that Uncle Walsh and Lucy were dating and that's what got them killed. What else could it be? Her and Miles's plans were going to fall apart before they even went on a date that was more than a few stolen moments in a coffee shop.

Neither of them talked about the summons when they got back in Miles's car, and they both actively ignored that he was driving them both to town hall until they were minutes away.

"I'll drop you off on the far side of the town hall park. There's a road that passes through a copse of trees where no one should be able to see us, but you'll have to walk about ten minutes," Miles said. He frowned as he spoke, but they both knew they couldn't be seen arriving together.

"Okay," she said, trying not to panic. Acting calm was going to be the key.

When he pulled to the side of the road to let her out, Miles turned to her. "We'll figure it out," he promised.

Jennifer looked him in the eye and nibbled on her lip. She wanted to believe him, but it was possible that this would be the last time they'd be able to see each other. Giving into the urge to kiss him, she leaned across the console and brushed her lips across his. His hand darted out and pulled her back for more of a kiss, making her heart race. She poured her heart into the kiss because if this was going to their only time, she wanted to make it last. When they broke apart, Miles's grin hit her like a ton of bricks.

"I can't wait to do that again," he whispered.

Blushing, Jennifer shifted into her hybrid form, her fluffy cream fur filling up the extra room in her cardigan. Not wanting to make their goodbye more painful, she reached for the door handle to leave.

Miles grabbed her arm. "Wait, my sweatshirt," Miles said. She'd been so flustered she'd forgotten she was wearing it.

Quickly, she stole another deep breath of his scent from the sweatshirt; then, she wriggled around and got the sweatshirt off in the small space of the car. She frowned at the black sweatshirt in her hands. "Maybe I should have taken it off before I shifted." She held it up, showing him it was covered in stray cream hairs. A few of the dark brown ones from her face and ears were there, too, but they were harder to see.

"Don't worry about it," Miles chuckled beside her, brushing his knuckles along her cheek. "I'll take care of it."

Jennifer tried to smile at him, but she must not have succeeded because he shook his head at her and urged her to go. She climbed out and headed to the path that led to her imminent doom.

Time stretched and shrank at the same time as town hall loomed larger and larger ahead of her. It wasn't the fanciest of places, but it was old and where city council meetings took place. It had one of those antiquated bells in a gazebo on the roof. Jennifer couldn't remember what it was called.

At the door, she refused to hesitate and look rattled. She went straight in and was relieved the entry was empty. Across the small entry way, she could already hear growls and hisses coming from inside the assembly room. On the other side of the door before her, her family would all be looking aloof or contemptuous. She needed to strive for aloofness. She wanted to turn around and leave, but she forced herself to walk in.

As soon as she entered, her mom waved her over to the front of the Capulet half of the room on the left. Jennifer hurried to her, ignoring the snarling Montagues on her right. Her heels clacked on the tile floor, and she felt like everyone knew she'd just been with Miles. She held her breath as her mom fussed over the "disaster" of her hair; she'd forgotten that Miles had mussed it in order to make her a little less Capulet perfect. At least her mom didn't notice that her lip gloss had been kissed off.

Over the next ten minutes, more of both families arrived, and two officers kept the families separated. Jennifer didn't know if the layout of the chairs — two arched groups with a large walkway between them — was strategic or just luck. She thought the two officers were vaguely familiar, but she wasn't sure if they were the ones from Felix's Corner or ones that she had seen when she went to the police station on Friday to talk to the detectives. She didn't say anything about them in case she recognized them from the latter. Still, she was happy they were there on the off chance her and Miles's dads tried to get into it again like they had at Felix's Corner.

For the hundredth time, she wished she hadn't texted her dad that day and passed on the information about Uncle Walsh and Lucy that she'd seen on Miles's phone. She should have let the police tell him, but she had been too upset to think straight.

She saw Miles come in after a bit. He was now wearing a red button up, but he hadn't done the top three buttons, so she could see that he'd just thrown it on over his blue shirt. He sat in the opposing front row with his parents, but turned around to talk with a group of golden retriever hybrids who she knew were his cousins. Miles was the only one of the Montague cousins who looked like he'd come from an office job even though he hadn't put his tie back on. His cousins were wearing athletic clothes, so they could have been doing something for the family company or just exercising before this.

The detectives finally arrived five minutes later, and they got everyone to quiet down.

"We've gathered everyone together," Detective Pinon started, "because what we've uncovered in our investigation affects both of your families."

"We'd like to make sure that any questions you might have about our findings are answered," Detective Barrdom finished.

Detective Pinon pulled an evidence bag out and approached Miles's dad. "We've done a handwriting analysis and determined that this is, without a doubt, Lucy Montague's handwriting. Do you concur?"

Miles's dad squinted at the slip of paper in the bag, started frowning deeply, and then nodded. "It is."

"We have fragments of several letters written by Lucy." The detective paused. "They are love letters."

The Montague section of the room started muttering to each other. Jennifer chanced a glance at Miles and saw he was looking at her, too, while a cousin whispered in his ear. It didn't seem like anyone in Miles's family knew that Lucy was dating someone.

"We only have fragments of these letters," Detective Barrdom continued over the Montagues, "because they were destroyed in the explosion at Walsh Capulet's townhouse."

The reaction was instantaneous. Both families stood up and started yelling. In all the noise, Jennifer wasn't sure if they were yelling at the detectives, at each other, across the walkway, or a combination thereof. Jennifer looked over at Miles again. They were the only ones sitting. Slowly, they both stood, maintaining eye contact. Jennifer wanted to think that Miles's eyes were trying to tell her they were still okay and that no one knew. But, once she was standing, her attention jerked to her mother next to her as she seethed, "I told him he was being an idiot and would regret it."

Ice pooled in Jennifer's veins and her head turned as if compelled. She looked at her mom. Really looked at her. Her mom had never been the warmest person, but Jennifer didn't want to believe *this*. Still, she couldn't think of any other explanation.

"You knew," Jennifer breathed the accusation.

Her mom rolled her eyes in response.

Suddenly, Jennifer found herself several feet away from her mom. She was now standing more with the detectives than her own family.

Jennifer repeated louder, "You knew."

Her sudden movement and words caught the attention of those who were standing closest to her and her mom. Soon, her whole family was looking at the two of them. It didn't take long for the Montagues to quiet down and watch too. Out of the corner of her eye, she saw Miles had taken a step or two toward her but was still firmly in his family's half of the room. His dad had grabbed his arm and stopped him from coming over to her.

"Fine," her mother huffed. She continued loud enough that both families could hear, "Yes, I knew. I told him to break it off, but he wouldn't listen to me."

Jennifer tried to slow down her panicked, gasping breaths. Her own mother? Could she have killed them?

"Did anyone else know?" Detective Pinon asked loudly.

Jennifer couldn't tear her eyes off her mom, but the shuffling of feet and whispers said that her mom was alone in her knowledge.

"Most of their relationship," Detective Barrdom said, "was conducted out of town. In Lucy Montague's case, she was on her typical road trips. In Walsh Capulet's case, he was either on a business trip or had time off from work."

"They did meet here in town," Detective Pinon added. "Not often, but on occasion, and only in their human forms in places that don't cater to hybrids. They were hoping to escape notice."

Jennifer felt like she couldn't breathe as she continued to stare at her mother. If Uncle Walsh and Lucy couldn't manage it, how could she and Miles?

Detective Barrdom continued: "However, with Nancy Capulet knowing about the relationship and the Montagues having Lucy followed, Walsh and Lucy knew they couldn't keep it up." Angry mutters on the Montague side of the room started at the "following" comment. They didn't like the insinuation that they would have someone in their family followed.

"Which is why," Detective Pinon bellowed over everyone, "they committed suicide together." His declaration brought a moment of silence.

"Suicide?" Miles asked.

Jennifer looked away from her mom and at the detectives. "No one in our families killed them?" she asked to be sure. Gasps greeted her question. The loudest of which came from her mom.

"No," Detective Barrdom said almost gently to her. "It was suicide." The detective focused back on the room at large then and explained, "We found witnesses from their last trip who saw them buy the plant that poisoned and killed Lucy, and while the poison wasn't strong enough to kill Walsh, he used a knife that Lucy had bought him on a different trip to finish the job. The bomb in Walsh's townhouse was made by them, using Lucy's camping propane tank as extra accelerant, and set off to destroy the love letters."

There was more talking and explanation, but Jennifer didn't hear any of it. She was recovering from the realization that her mother hadn't murdered her uncle. As the volume rose and arguments started within each family group and across the walkway between the families, Jennifer looked over at Miles. He shook off his dad's hold and walked over to her.

"Hey," Miles said quietly once he was right in front of her. "Looks like we're not likely to be murdered. That's got to be worth something, right?"

Jennifer felt her tears slide into the fur on her cheeks. She didn't know if they were tears of relief that Miles was right or tears of sadness that Uncle Walsh and Lucy felt like they'd had no other choice because of their families.

"What did you say to her to make her cry?" Jennifer's mom said sharply to Miles.

Glaring through her tears at her mom, Jennifer stepped right beside Miles and leaned into him. She felt him wrap his arm around her, and the voices in the room fell silent one by one. Several faces among both their families were aghast, some were shocked, and a few of the younger family members were split between amused smiles and sympathetic "good luck" winces.

"I'd suggest," Detective Barrdom said from behind them, "that both families give these two their support."

Miles's arm tightened around her as they watched their families exchange glances and then quietly start talking amongst themselves. No one said anything for or against them, but they kept glancing their way.

"So, rabid animosity is over?" Detective Pinon said. His voice was so bright that they all turned their attention to him. "Great." He looked at Detective Barrdom and asked, "Poppy, can I take you out to dinner?"

"Uh," the detective blinked in surprise at her partner and then smiled. "Sure."

After a while, the family members started to slowly leave, and Jennifer heard Detective Barrdom quietly say to Detective Pinon, "Do you think this will solve your problem?"

"It might. I'll argue that I was trying to fight my attraction to you and play a role for the Montagues. Either way, I get to take the Spoville Police Department's prettiest detective out on a date." Detective Pinon's smug smile made Jennifer hide her face in Miles's shoulder to muffle her laugh. Maybe they'd all get the happily ever after that Uncle Walsh and Lucy never had the chance at.

Epilogue

Bill

Bill didn't want the theater lights to come on when the credits finished rolling. Kim was curled up under his arm with her feet tucked up on the seat under her dress. After the explosion in the movie scared her into shifting, she'd been adorably fluffy against him. He'd made a point of not looking at her right after she'd shifted. He knew she was self-conscious about it. Anyone who stayed in their human form as much as they physically could had to be self-conscious about their hybrid form. At least in Granberg, since no one cared what someone's hybrid form looked like.

He'd only seen Kim in her hybrid form once before. In Sculpture I, someone had dropped their project and screamed like they were being stabbed, startling Kim into shifting. Bill had thought she looked adorable even back then with her fluffy white fur sticking every which way and her wide, dark brown eyes. It had taken him almost two years to work up enough guts to ask her out. He'd seen her around campus here and there, but none of their friends overlapped.

He had never dated much, since he was too nerdy to catch anyone's eyes, or that's what he told himself. Really, he knew women could be into nerdy, but he still lacked the confidence of a tomcat. He didn't want Kim to figure out yet just how socially awkward he could be. Or that he'd had to switch his enrollment in Sculpture I from a graded class to pass/fail (and barely convinced the professor not to fail him). Though she might already know that since he'd been terrible at sculpture.

Bill knew he'd beat himself up if graduation came and went, and he'd never taken the risk of at least asking Kim out. So, in the end, he'd just walked across the campus quad to where she was reading a book on a blanket in the sun and asked her out.

Tonight, it had killed him a little to pretend that he hadn't even noticed that she'd shifted, but when he didn't react, she didn't shift back! Once she finally relaxed and seemed engrossed in the movie, he'd been able to steal a glance at her. She was gorgeous in both her skins.

Still, when the credits ended, he felt the fur on her arm under the pads of his fingers slide away and disappear. She moved slightly away from him and slid her feet back into her sandals on the ground before anyone could trip on them. The lights slowly grew brighter in the room, and Kim smiled shyly at him.

Bill leaned in like he had a secret and quietly said, "I thought we could get dessert and talk about the movie." Kim nodded and let him take her hand as they walked out of the theater.

They went to a little bakery nearby that Bill had scoped out in advance. He ordered a cinnamon roll, and Kim got a tuna croissant. The little table in the back corner, away from the front windows, was open, and Bill made sure that they sat there. It was partially secluded and struck him as cozy.

"What did you think?" Kim asked once they'd each taken a bite of their pastries.

"It definitely lived up to the hype," he told her. "It was *Romeo and Juliet*, but totally different. That Miles and Jenny weren't the doomed match isn't what I expected even once their aunt and uncle were found dead."

"Yeah, it didn't occur to me that the older characters were the actual Romeo and Juliet of the movie. I also liked how it was more of the background story, and we got the detective story as the focus. That made it stand apart from the original, too."

"I wanted to see more of Miles and Jenny's secret coffee shop dates. Their story had really hooked me at the start of the movie," Bill said. He didn't tell her that he thought she looked a little like Connie Prince who played Jenny Capulet with all the soft fluffiness of fur. She probably wouldn't believe him. Especially if he admitted that her nose was way cuter than the actress's.

"That would have been fun," Kim agreed. Bill watched her teeth sink into her croissant as she took another bite. A blush rose in her cheeks, and Bill realized he was staring. And she'd noticed.

"What about you? Were there other parts you wanted more of?" he asked, looking down at his half-eaten roll in order to stop staring.

"Apollo's house fascinated me. I loved how it was over-the-top. I've been thinking that I might install a scratching post in my next place," Kim said quietly as if embarrassed. "But I haven't seen homes that are truly set up to accommodate the type of hybrid someone is. Do you think that will start happening like in the movie?"

"Definitely," Bill said. "My freshman-year roommate studied architecture and has done some internships with architects. He's seen plans to make homes that are half aquarium and told me about the progress on making mini biospheres to recreate habitats for zoos. He thinks that, in the future, some of the more sensitive hybrids might use them to create environments around their homes that are perfectly suited for them."

Kim blinked at him in shock, her mouth hanging open a little. Bill swallowed hard. He hadn't meant to geek out on her, but the way the world was changing and what it would do to history over time was a bit of an obsession for him.

"Wow," she finally said.

"And you should definitely get a scratching post in your next place," he added before he could stop himself. "I love mine."

She gifted him with another sweet smile that he didn't think he deserved.

"It would have been cool to see where Poppy and Apollo's story went," Kim said, returning to the safe topic of the movie.

"I heard that they're already in negotiations to make a sequel," Bill informed her.

"Do you think they started considering it before this one hit theaters with a bang?"

"If they did test screenings, probably. I don't think the movie industry realized how big it would be to have a movie, any movie, in which almost all the actors took their hybrid forms. It was awesome to see that on screen."

"It made it look like Granberg won't be an eye-sore in the future. It might be the model for other areas."

"Hybrids are the majority now," Bill agreed. "It makes sense that our hybrid forms will be more and more accepted."

"That would be nice," she said quietly.

He wondered what she was thinking. Was she thinking about being accepted with all her fur? If she spent more time in her hybrid form, she'd see that, in Granberg at least, she already would be. For them, the future of acceptance was already there. She just needed to embrace it.

"In any case, we should definitely go see the sequel when it comes out."

Bill froze. He couldn't believe he'd just said that. The sequel wouldn't come out for at least a year, if that soon. What was she going to think? This was their first date.

"Maybe we will," she said with a giggle before he could completely freak out.

"Maybe we will," he repeated back to her with a smile.

I hope you enjoyed reading *Opposites Collide*! If you want to keep reading more in this world, sign up for my newsletter on my website to get a free story about life and love when the Crisis hit and everyone changed, updates on my next book, and more: https://daysgrant.com/contact-2/

If you haven't already, check out book 1 in The Mavens series, *Touchy Talents*, which takes place thirty years after *Opposites Collide* (the movie) came out. In The Mavens, you'll see the *Opposites Collide* movie, its sequels, and actors pop up from time to time. You'll even see Kim and Bill's kids! Get your copy of *Touchy Talents* here: https://books.daysgrant.com/og2ux1l64v

About the Author

Day S. Grant's debut series is The Mavens, but she has other series that are fighting to be written next. Her story ideas all start from a single scene she saw in a dream, and they grow and evolve from there.

Her fascination with the other has grown throughout her life. She believes that things aren't as different as they seem. Her books consistently introduce opposites, others, and new perspectives that shift how people see the world.

A traveler at heart, when Day S. isn't traveling through the pages of a book with a steaming cup of tea, she is exploring new places. She loves nature and likes finding interesting trees to photograph. When she can, she takes her cats with her on her adventures.

Her passion for creating isn't contained to the blank page, but also manifests in doodles and in a life-long sewing hobby. She enjoys making clothes for herself and, on occasion, for her very patient cats.

Learn more about Day S. Grant and her upcoming releases by signing up for her newsletter on her website: www.daysgrant.com/contact-2/

Acknowledgements

I'd like to thank Belinda, Jen, Laural, Maggie, and my dad for finding the holes in my story. Without their help, I would undoubtably have overlooked key aspects of the story (like who would think to put a lawyer in a detective story? not me...!).

This story would have taken much longer to get out if I didn't have the Author Ever After community behind me as I moved from the writing journey to the publishing journey. Those are definitely two very different things, but a book doesn't get completed without both parts. I'm immensely grateful for the tips and quick answers to all my publishing questions.

I'd also like to thank my editors Kelly and Brit for taking a close look at my writing and making it the best it can be. Their work let me take a step away from my story and see the words that built it.

Also by Day S. Grant

The Mavens

Touchy Talents

Shell Shocked (coming 2026)

In the Mavens' world

Opposites Collide

Opposites Clash (coming 2026)